I0760414

REDEEMED

A STORY OF GRACE, SECOND CHANCES, AND LOVE'S POWER TO HEAL

THE ADOPTED SERIES
BOOK FOUR

MEGGAN LARSON

Library and Archives Canada Cataloguing in Publications.

For permissions contact:

hello@starfishstoriespublishing.com

E-Book ISBN: 978-1-990419-62-1

Print ISBN: 978-1-990419-63-8

Dust Jacket ISBN: 978-1-990419-64-5

1st Edition

Edited by C.B. Moore

Cover Designed by Meraki Cover Design

For Rob - my real life Lucas
(who the character has always been based on).

1

OLIVIA

"*Aren't you Olivia Jackson?"*

I cringed internally before turning and smiling at the high school girl who had just tapped me on the shoulder. She had such large curious eyes brimming with excitement, I felt like I was about to be studied under a microscope. "Yeah, that's me," I replied with a small smile while bracing myself for what always came next.

"Oh my gosh, I knew it! Are you still running? I thought you were heading to the Olympics after all those commercials you were doing."

She looked at me expectantly and I took a deep, shuddering breath, silently cursing my boss once again for insisting I do this event.

Blowing out my breath, I spoke fast to get it over with. "I shattered my ankle during my last race so, uh… I'm not Olympic bound anymore."

The girl's shoulders slumped and her mouth turned down. "Damn, girl, I was such a big fan. You'll get back out there though, right?" She looked so hopeful I almost felt guilty.

My fingernails dug into my palms, distracting me from the

burden of what I was about to say. "Nah, I can't compete anymore." I cleared my throat, desperate to change the subject. "Will you be going to Florida U?" I pointed to the giant banner welcoming prospective athletes.

She shrugged. "Maybe, I'm keeping my options open. It was nice to meet you, Olivia."

Before she turned to walk away, our eyes met and I saw the same thing everyone showed when they found out my track career was over: pity. The anger that had become my constant companion as of late burned deep within me like a lake of fire consuming every good thing in its path. It was almost comforting to feel it stirring. It was so familiar to me now, I was sure I'd feel its loss were it ever to disappear.

Everything was going according to plan—at least for the event. Dozens of tables filled the hotel ballroom, each draped with a white tablecloth and topped with a vase of fresh flowers. It was a full house, which I knew would please my boss. Almost as if I had summoned her, she suddenly appeared by my side, her voice low in my ear.

"This couldn't be going any better. Every table is full, and at $250 a plate, the university is going to be very happy."

"That's great, Carrie. I'm sure this will be good for business," I said.

"Your dad was right about you. You're a total natural at this whole event-planning thing. It's like you were born for it." She squeezed my arm and I watched her head backstage to triple check the guest speakers were ready.

Like you were born for it. Her words bounced around my brain like a pinball. *Born for event planning? Please. I was born to run.* I didn't mean to be ungrateful. Jason had really hooked me up when I needed a job, but it was supposed to keep my mind off track, not make me plan an event for a life I'd never have again. Glancing around, I decided I wasn't needed right at that moment, so I snuck over to the restroom for a little break. Once inside, I took advantage of the chair strategically placed by the sinks and slunk down into it. I slipped my left foot out of my black flat and rubbed my throbbing ankle.

It didn't bother me nearly as much as it had eighteen months ago when the accident happened, but if I stood for too long, I was quickly reminded of why my running days were behind me. Of why my carefully crafted plans of sponsorships, eventual coaching and broadcasting, and even commentating for the summer Olympics—after winning gold, of course—were over. One moment. One tiny miscalculation, and I fell. I was still falling, to be honest with myself, but I didn't like to do that all too often.

I slid my foot back into my shoe and stood to glance at my reflection in the large round mirror backlit with fancy lighting to ensure I was still presentable. The bright yellow dress I wore hung just below my knees, popping out with a slight flare at the bottom. I'd worn it because it was vibrant and happy, hoping it would mask what I felt on the inside. Swept to the side, my hair tumbled down the front of my shoulder, held in place by an obscene amount of bobby pins and hair spray. They seemed to be doing their job, as not a strand was out of place. At least that I could control. I nodded like I was giving myself a pre-race talk and then returned to the ballroom quickly to take my place beside the stage just as the speeches began.

There was lots of schmoozing and encouraging the largesse of pocketbooks, and even a nod to my boss's company, Indigo Events, for putting together such a fabulous evening. Carrie practically vibrated with joy beside me and her laugh, the sound big and booming, made her face light up and her generous bosom nod in agreement. The university was raising money for their track and cross-country programs to entice Olympic hopefuls to train at their school through scholarships. Carrie was right, I was the best person to plan this event, but being in a room full of athletes and coaches was serving as a stark reminder of what I had lost.

"Miss Jackson?" A man in a suit with salt and pepper hair lightly touched my arm.

"Yes?" I whispered back as someone on stage clicked through a slide deck of previous competitions won.

"I thought that was you," he replied with a smile. "I haven't seen you in any local commercials lately. Don't tell me you've retired already." He gripped his chest in mock devastation as I plastered a smile on my face.

"Not by choice," I murmured softly and pointed to the presentation as an excuse for why I couldn't continue to chat. He squinted and I turned before I could see the pity I knew was written all over his face.

Carrie glanced at her watch and gave me a nod of dismissal. She could handle things from there, and I was free to get to the party I was missing.

"Shot! Shot! Shot! Shot!"

The crowd surrounding me cheered as I downed my fourth shot in a row and bit down hard on the lemon wedge I shoved into my mouth.

"Olivia, I'm so glad we met all that time ago."

I looked at the girl who had spoken, trying to remember her name. She was drunk and slurring her words. We had met a few weeks before at another event Indigo had hosted, but I had her in my phone as "cool girl from duck race," so I had been referring to her as Duckie in my mind.

"Me too Du…girl," I clapped her on the shoulder and went to the bar to get another drink.

"Can I see some ID?" The bartender looked like he was maybe twenty-five; he had dark hair and the kind of piercing blue eyes that could make me forget I was sad.

I fished my driver's license out of the tiny purse I wore across my chest and silently handed it over.

"Twenty-two huh? I wouldn't have pegged you for legal yet," he said with a smirk.

"I get that a lot," I replied, matching his energy with a flirtatious smile.

He handed me my screwdriver and let his fingers linger over mine for a beat longer than was necessary. I took a sip as I swayed along to the music pumping through the room.

"I haven't seen you here before," he said loudly in an effort to be heard.

"First time. What even is this place?" I let my eyes wander to the high ceilings and exposed wooden beams.

"It used to be a barn then some rich guy converted it into… this." He gestured to the massive space.

"Cool," I responded with a shrug.

His gaze raked over me and he leaned in. "You wanna dance?"

"Aren't you working?" I giggled.

He nodded to the other bartender and pointed to the dance floor then hopped over the bar. "I'm on a break now." His lips were against my ear as he gently guided me to the dance floor.

I swallowed the last of my drink and then his hands were on my hips, pulling me closer as we danced. After a few minutes, he tilted my chin up and I didn't stop him from kissing me.

It was how it always went. Meet cute guy, flirt, he kisses me, I let him, then I go home alone. Rinse and repeat. The truth was, I hadn't ever slept with anyone. I'd always wanted my first time to be with Lucas, and no one had ever compared. Keeping my extra curriculars in public was how I stayed in control, and I had no intention of relinquishing that to anyone.

As if on cue, he got closer and murmured, "Want to get out of here?"

I shook my head. "I've gotta go."

The alcohol was making my head feel light, and I figured I was another drink or two away from making worse life decisions. He gave me a business card and I politely thanked him, then headed out into the night air to catch an Uber back to my apartment. My phone buzzed with a text from my adoptive dad signaling to me that it was almost midnight. It was the only time he messaged me, and neither of us mentioned why that was.

I miss you. I understand why you're keeping your distance, but I do miss you.

I HEARTED the message and replied.

Miss you too.

AS I SCROLLED through our messages I smiled at the memes and GIFs he had sent over the months. My smile faded as I tapped onto my mom's messages and saw that the last one had been from six months ago, reminding me about the money I owed them.

I sighed and paid my fare, heading into the crappy apartment I shared with a roommate. Kicking off my shoes, I stumbled into my room. My gaze slid over to the picture I kept on my dresser of G.G. and me the day I was allowed to visit her again. We wore the biggest grins and my hand was over hers, squeezing it tightly. My whole world had felt like it had finally been coming together then.

Opening my top drawer, I dropped the bartender's business card on a stack of others, careful not to look at the necklace in the corner.

Dropping on my bed fully clothed, I let my mind wander as I welcomed the heaviness attempting to pull me under. His face drifted into my mind like always, and I wondered how he was. Did he ever think of me? Did he miss me? *Get over it, Liv. If he wanted you, he would have stayed in touch.*

I covered my eyes with my arm and whispered to myself in the dark, "The loves of your life are gone, and it's time to move on." I'd said it so often it had become like a nursery rhyme in my mind. I knew I'd forget him eventually. I had to. After all, it wasn't like I was ever going to see him again.

2

LUCAS

Had it always been this sunny? It's not like I hadn't been outside in two years, but I was used to the barbed-wire fence preventing me from leaving.

Being on this side of the doors was surreal. So was wearing my own clothes again. A bead of sweat trickled down my back and I searched the parking lot. I snorted as I found my brother Dylan leaning up against his rust-bucket piece-of-crap Mazda, smoking a cigarette. He acknowledged my existence with a nod and I returned it.

Relief flooded through me. *He actually showed up.* I jogged across the parking lot to meet him. We weren't exactly close, so I wasn't gonna throw my arms around him or anything, but it was nice that he hadn't flaked for once.

"Hey, convict," he said with a smirk.

"That's ex-convict, thanks." My voice sounded weird in my ears. I'd spent more time writing than talking for the last two years.

"You're all muscle now. Looks like you went in a boy and came out a man." He laughed at his own joke while I got used to the brightness of the outside world. "Whatcha got there?"

He eyed the stack of composition notebooks in my arms.

They'd been like a lifeline to me while I tried to stay under the radar and keep to myself in there. Not that I was about to tell him that.

"Don't worry about it. You almost done? As much as I'd love to hang out in the parking lot of the prison all day..."

"Good to know some things never change," he said as he dropped his cigarette on the ground and twisted his foot over it.

He punched my shoulder, nearly causing me to drop my notebooks, and we got into his car. It started after a few tries and I let out a sigh of relief as we finally left behind the place I'd called home for two years.

Aside from my wallet, clothes, and disconnected phone, the only other thing the guard had handed me back as I left was the letter Liv had written me. I had read it so many times that it was seared into my memory, but I still pulled it out to look at it again.

Dear Lucas, I love you. I should have told you that day on the beach when you said it to me. I've regretted that moment ever since. It never mattered to me where or how you grew up. You'll never be trash to me. Exactly the opposite, actually. You are the boy who helped me find myself when I was lost beyond recognition. I hope that someday I can help you do the same.

Love, Liv

I COULD STILL PICTURE every inch of her. Those green eyes, cute little nose, pouty lips that I could kiss all day, long dark hair that she usually straightened but had been curly the last time I'd seen her—and it had taken all my self-control not to run my hands through it and pull her close.

"What's that?" My brother's voice broke through my thoughts.

I quickly folded up the letter and put it in my pocket. "Nothing," I mumbled while staring out the window.

"You and your secrets," he said knowingly.

I glanced at him as he drove. Though at twenty-eight he was only five years my senior, he looked much older. We were brothers but looked nothing alike—except for our eyes. His face was flushed and puffy, and his crowfeet prominent; his dark hair was unkempt and dull.

"You good, man? You're looking a little...rough." I tried to keep the worry out of my voice, but as usual he saw right through me.

"Worried about me, little brother?" he joked. "I'm fine, just a little tired from work."

"You still working at the bar?"

"Yeah, I manage it now." He cleared his throat to mask the pride I knew was there.

"That's cool," I replied, and punched his arm to relieve the tension. We didn't do emotions too well in our family.

"I can give you a job if you want."

"I think I should probably stay away from too much alcohol," I mused. It hadn't done me any favors.

"Right. Well, you can stay with me while you figure things out. I've got a pullout couch with your name on it." He laughed.

"Thanks, man."

I looked out the window as we weaved in and out of the Florida traffic. A Corvette flew in front of us, causing my brother to slam on the brakes and my notebooks to go sprawling to my feet. He swore and flipped off the driver as she proceeded to cut off every lane and barely make the exit. *This, I didn't miss.*

Signs for a familiar exit began popping up, and without thinking I asked my brother to get off the highway.

"Here?" he asked even as he took the exit.

"Turn left at the lights."

It was a mistake. I knew that, but I couldn't stop giving him directions to Liv's parents' place. We parked across the street, and for a split second I imagined myself going up to the door, ringing the bell, and asking where she was. But I wouldn't—couldn't, really.

The tree in their yard, once large and full of life, was just a stump now. There were no cars in the driveway, and the basketball net hung above the garage was missing most of its netting and looked abandoned. The paint on the garage was chipping and looked due for a new coat soon.

I'd never forgotten the way her mother glared at me in that courtroom, silently blaming me—for what, I wasn't sure. Probably not being good enough for her daughter, which was definitely accurate. She'd never liked me, and she turned out to be right. I didn't deserve Liv. Not after the way I'd treated her and then disappeared on her and all my friends. Only my brother knew where I'd been for the last two years of my life. Well, Nate too.

And no one needed an ex-con in their life—especially Liv.

"Who lives here?" My brother turned to me with curiosity on his face.

I shrugged, feigning indifference. "Just someone I used to know."

"Right. Why is the garage purple?"

I smiled to myself at the memory of Liv as she complained about her dad painting their garage purple and making all the neighbors hate them. I shrugged again.

"Okay, then. Are you going in or just gonna stalk the outside of her house like a creep?" The laughter in his voice made me want to wipe the smile off his face and I hated that his assumption of the house's occupant being a "her" was right.

"Nah, we can go." I looked away as we drove off, not wanting to be the guy who gazed forlornly at his ex's house, wishing things had worked out differently. Only, that was exactly who I was.

We got to my brother's dingy apartment—and though I was grateful for a place to stay, I took one look at his pull-out couch with complimentary burn holes and stains and decided I needed to get my own place as soon as possible. Dishes were piled up in the kitchen sink, looking so dirty I thought they might grow legs and walk away. His clothes lay strewn about the apartment carelessly, and everything smelled like cigarettes.

He clapped me on the back and headed to his room. "Home sweet home," he called behind him, then added, "Dish soap is under the sink."

I shook my head as though to dispel my thoughts while mentally making a list of what I needed to do. *Reactivate cell phone. Go to the career center for help getting a job. Get job, get paid, secure place for myself, move out.*

But first, I surveyed the mess before me and tucked my things into the corner of the couch.

Clean up this mess.

3

OLIVIA

"Oh, you scoundrel!" G.G.'s finger wagged in my face as I took the last trick and euchred her after she had called hearts as trump.

"I'm not sorry, G.G. If you're gonna call trump in Euchre you'd better have the cards to back it up," I said with a laugh.

"Well, I thought I could count on Matteo here to win at least *one* hand," she muttered.

"Sorry, my love, I had nothing but black." Matteo walked around the small courtyard table and kissed my great-grandmother on the cheek.

She popped a piece of shrimp—loaded with sauce, of course—into her mouth and grumbled to herself as she glared at me. "Why can't we have table talk? He could have warned me!"

I laughed harder. "Because that's against the rules." I waggled my eyebrows at my sister Leah, who sat beside G.G. and had been trying to hold her laughter in since "you scoundrel."

Every Tuesday evening at 6:30 p.m., the four of us had a standing date to play cards at the assisted living facility where G.G. lived. I got off work at five p.m. and had just enough time to head over. Leah had joined us from the time she and her dad moved closer after her parents split up.

I snuck a glance at her and marveled at the fact that I was hanging out with members of my biological family. She looked a bit like me, with a small nose and green eyes. Her skin was much paler than mine and her hair was a very light brown, but to look at us, you could guess that we might be related. It was all I'd ever wanted, and here we were playing Euchre together.

"How did you get so good at this game?" Matteo playfully bumped his shoulder against mine. He, too, lived at the facility, and he and G.G. had been smitten with each other ever since he moved in.

"My adoptive dad taught me everything I know," I said with a smile. It was true, but our risk aversions were at very different levels. That man would go all in playing poker on a queen and a nine, whereas I'd hesitate with a flush because it wasn't a royal flush. It was like I always expected someone else to swoop in with the upper hand.

G.G.'s sparkly pink top shimmered as the sky changed to gorgeous shades of pink and orange in the setting mid-September sun. I never tired of watching the sky transform before my eyes. We played a few more hands while G.G. got increasingly more sarcastic until Matteo couldn't take it anymore.

"Ruth, my love, you are getting so worked up. Let's go inside and have a hot drink."

He gestured to the inside sitting area as he unlocked the brakes on her wheelchair, and Leah and I trailed behind them. His thick Italian accent was, I suspected, one of the many reasons why G.G. was so smitten. The other reasons likely had to do with his salt and pepper hair, so thick you could get lost in it, and blue eyes that made you never want to look away. He was like a senior Italian model, and he clearly loved her. I smiled to myself as I watched them.

We drank tea and ate cookies though it was over eighty

degrees. The air conditioning was kept surprisingly low, and I noticed many of the residents curled up with blankets. I made a mental note to mention it to the manager the next time I saw her.

"So, my sweet Olivia, your best friend is finally marrying that nice boy, yes?" G.G. dunked her cookie into the cup of tea in front of her and took a dainty bite.

"Yes, she is. Their engagement party is in a few weeks," I said as I took a sip of my London Fog. The kitchen staff were the best at Tuscan Gardens, and when they found out how much I loved London Fogs they made a point to serve me one every time I stopped by.

"I'm so happy for them," Leah said as she bounced on her seat with excitement. "Will you be planning the party?"

I shook my head. "No, I've been forbidden from organizing anything. Her and Nate didn't want me to have to work during their party, so they're having it at his parents' club." Mela had been outraged by my suggestion to have Indigo handle the party. Then she had—astutely—accused me of wanting to hide behind work to avoid socializing.

"She knows you well," G.G. said with a smirk as though reading my mind.

"I have no idea what you're talking about," I murmured while taking another sip of my drink. "You're all invited, by the way. You should be getting your invitations in the mail this week."

"Me too?" Leah asked with her eyes downcast.

I touched her arm lightly. "Of course, you're family."

She met my eyes, and a moment of understanding passed between us. My tumultuous relationship with our shared mother had nothing to do with my relationship with her, and I wasn't about to let it affect our friendship. Relief sparked in her eyes as I gave her a slight nod. We might not have grown up together, but our sibling connection was intact. Just like with Mela, we could share a look and speak volumes without saying a word.

"How is your senior year going, Leah?" Matteo asked while

G.G. wiped at her misty eyes, no doubt having noticed the silent conversation between her great-granddaughters.

"I mean, it's only been a couple of weeks, but so far so good. I was kind of worried about starting my senior year at a new school in a new city, but honestly, living with my dad has been so chill that it's made all the change pretty manageable."

Out of the corner of my eye I saw G.G. purse her lips and threw her a sympathetic gaze. Last year Leah had tried to take her life with pills, and when Ali tried to sweep it under the rug instead of getting Leah some much needed support, that was the final straw for Mark, who filed for divorce a week after Leah was released from the hospital. G.G. was still pissed—understandably—and I wasn't sure if she'd ever really forgive Ali. It felt weird for her to be on the outs and me to be part of the inner circle, but I wasn't complaining.

We chatted for a while longer and promptly at eight p.m. Leah and I stood to give hugs and leave. Matteo pulled me into his arms, kissed both my cheeks, and called me *bellissima* as always. He did the same to Leah, whose face flushed at the compliment.

When I leaned over to give G.G. a hug, she pulled me—with surprising force—down into the chair beside her.

"Olivia, I need you to remember something, okay? You can still find love and contentment in things and in people, even if they've changed," she started.

"Okay…" I wasn't sure where she was going with this, and my stomach flipped with uneasiness.

"I'm just saying, there's no sense crying over spilled milk. Yes, your running career is over." She put a finger in the air to stop me from interrupting, so I closed my mouth. "I see the sadness in you, sweetheart, even though you try to hide it from me." I grimaced as she went on. "I never would have imagined the happiness I've found with Matteo, but that joy was only possible because of loss. I lost my husband, I lost my health, and then I lost my freedom, being locked away in a place that stiffs me on shrimp sauce every day." I laughed as I wiped a tear from my eye. "You can still find beauty in life even if and when the path is different than you thought it would be."

My defenses melted and I rested my head on her lap as she held me tightly, the same way she had the day we met. Her words were a lighthouse guiding me to the shore after my drowning in a sea of regret. I felt...seen. G.G. had lost so much over the years, and I knew she was honest to a fault. She wouldn't say something just to fluff me up. I looked at her, and I was sure her watery smile matched my own.

"Thank you, G.G. I love you," I whispered.

"I love you right back, my sweet girl."

4

LUCAS

I walked into The Glen and breathed a sigh of relief when I saw Nate at a booth waving me over. The grin on his face was contagious and I was grateful that he was a water-under-the-bridge kind of friend. His vintage Smashing Pumpkins t-shirt was obviously meant for someone twice his size, and it hung down over his board shorts.

"Hey, man, long time no see." He stood and pulled me into a hug, clapping me hard on the back.

"Yeah, it's been a minute. It's good to see you," I said with an easy smile, sliding into the booth across from him.

"Damn, dude, you're like twice the size you were before you left. Did you do anything besides work out?"

"Not really, no." I laughed. Being with Nate had always been effortless, and I was grateful that hadn't changed after two years.

A waitress came by to take our order—the same as always: beer and fish and chips. The place was technically a Scottish pub-slash-restaurant, and it was where Nate and I used to hang out a lot. It had moved from a tiny hole in the wall with the tables practically on top of each other to a fancier space with huge windows, outdoor dining, sleek tables and leather chairs.

The pub was great, but it was the ownership that really made the atmosphere impossible to resist. A family-owned business for nearly forty years, complete with trivia nights, karaoke, and dog days on the patio every Monday. They welcomed everyone as family—even pets.

"Let's get this over with, Luke." Nate leaned back in his seat expectantly.

Instead of playing dumb and pretending I had no clue what he was talking about, I got right to it. "Thanks for keeping in touch while I was…on vacation."

He laughed out loud. "Is that what they're calling it these days?"

"Har-har," I replied sarcastically, then went on. "Seriously, writing letters isn't something I ever would have expected from you, but damn if it didn't make the time pass just a little bit faster. So, uh, thanks. I appreciated it." I cleared my throat, hoping to rid myself of the knot in it.

"Well, I would have just emailed you like someone in this century, but since you went dark on all socials, it was that or smoke signals, and I just wasn't sure you'd see them." His blue eyes twinkled.

"You're an ass." I laughed again.

He snatched a fry from my plate and popped it into his mouth while I took a long pull of my beer.

"How's Mela?" My voice faltered unexpectedly. The last time I'd heard, Mela was still best friends with Liv, and the latter was off limits to ask about.

Nate looked uneasy for the first time since I'd walked in. "She's fine. Good. But, uh, she doesn't know about your little 'vacation'." He said the word with air quotes.

My eyebrows rose in surprise. "You didn't tell her? Why not?"

He shrugged while he dipped his fish into the sauce on his plate. "Wasn't my secret to tell, I guess."

"Nate, I never would have expected you to keep something like that from her. I'm sorry you felt you had to." Part of me had hoped he would tell her so she'd tell Liv. Somehow that seemed easier than her thinking I had just disappeared for two years.

"It's fine, man. But you need to keep this between us now because if she finds out that I hid something this huge, she may back out of marrying me." His eyes were trained on me, gauging my reaction.

"Wait, what? You're getting *married*?" When the hell had that happened?

His smile said it all. "She's the love of my life. Of course I'm marrying her. I want you to be my best man." I started to protest and he waved me off. "Don't give me some self-deprecating BS about how you're not good enough blah, blah, blah. I don't wanna hear it, Luke."

Glaring at him, I stayed quiet and took another swig of my beer. He knew exactly how I'd feel about his request. I'd treated him like crap when I was spiraling and then was MIA for a year and a half *before* I went to prison.

"Come on, you must have other friends who won't bring a rap sheet to the reception," I joked uneasily.

"Yeah, I do. But you're the brother I never had. It's not like I've spent a bunch of time dreaming about my wedding or anything, but when I picture it, you're the one standing there. So, get over whatever pity party this is and just say yes already." He sighed into his next bite like my presence was exhausting him. Maybe it was.

I wanted to say yes; I did. But there was one giant problem I wasn't sure he'd thought of yet. "Who's Mela's maid of honor?" I asked folding my arms over my chest, knowing exactly what the answer would be.

"Ah, yeah. About that," he started. "You need to patch things up with Liv."

Hearing her name made my heart contract so suddenly I winced. "That's a tall order, my friend. Unless you're getting married in"—I checked my watch for dramatic effect—"about twenty years, I don't think that's happening."

"You can start at the engagement party in a few weeks." He smirked into his beer as my jaw dropped.

I shook my head. "No. There's no way I'm going to that." Nate had officially lost his mind.

"I won't tell Mela you're coming."

"Oh, that should go over well."

"If I tell her, she might hire security to work the doors and keep you out." I wasn't sure whether he was kidding. "You screwed up, big time. We both know that. We also know that you never got over Liv—and now that you're both living in the same place again, you're not going to be able to avoid her forever."

"She lives *here*? What happened to New York? To running?" She'd had her dreams all worked out, it seemed. I couldn't imagine what would have brought her back home.

"It's not my place to tell her story," he said with another shrug.

"I'm gonna start calling you the vault." His face lit up like I'd praised him.

"I'll text you the details later. As my best man—"

"I haven't accepted yet."

Annoyance flashed across his face. "As my best man, you need to be there. So do your little meditations or whatever else you learned on 'vacation' and get your head in the game."

"I'm not going, Nate. I can't face her. Not after everything I did."

"No risk, no reward, brother." He tossed a few bills on the table, punched me in the shoulder, and strode out of the pub like he'd just dropped a mic.

"Dammit," I muttered to myself as I finished my beer and walked out after him.

I LEANED back against the couch and hit send on the twentieth job application of the night. My brother had gone out on what I assumed was a date judging by the careless trail of clothing that led out of his bedroom door and littered the floor—again. I had to get my own place.

Having applied for every job I could think of, I closed my brother's laptop and cracked open a beer, deciding which movie I was going to fall asleep to on my newly reactivated phone thanks to Nate's insistence on paying the bill. He was also the reason my dilapidated car was back on the road. I owed him, as usual.

In pajama pants and a white t-shirt, I let my thumb hover over the Netflix app, but then I tapped on Instagram instead. I knew it was a mistake to look her up, but I couldn't seem to stop myself. No one would ever know anyway.

I found her account quickly and scrolled through her pictures. She'd posted one a few days ago, and her face was radiant as she looked into the camera and smiled. Her golden skin was glowing and her curls fell on one side and down the front of her shoulder. It looked like she was wearing a yellow tank top or a dress and there was a crowd of people behind her. Her green eyes shone with laughter.

Another picture had the caption, "Work, work, work." and she had tagged Indigo Events. I guessed that's where she was working now. There was no trace of anything to do with running on her account. It made me curious, though I had no right to be. She looked happy and seemed to have new friends. She got tagged in a lot of pictures.

One of the pictures was taken from a distance, and she was smiling while talking to a guy with her hand on his arm. The jealousy that twisted in my gut made me want to throw up. Was that her boyfriend? *It's none of your damn business,* I chided myself.

Business or not, I hated seeing these pictures of her without me. I rubbed my chest to ease the pain that had just manifested. I finished my third beer of the night. Maybe I'd drunk them too fast because all of a sudden the alcohol was making decisions for me.

Before I knew it, I was texting Nate back to tell him I'd be his best man and go to his engagement party. He sent me a slew of expletives and emojis, making me laugh and lightening the heaviness that had been growing in me.

I felt the flush of regret nipping at the edges of my mind. *I can always leave before she sees me.* There, it was settled then. I'd go—for Nate, obviously. What kind of a friend would I be if I didn't agree to be there for him on the most important day of his life?

5

OLIVIA

I hadn't seen her since the trial, yet here she was, sitting across from me at Perkins, having bribed me out of bed early on a Saturday morning with the promise of a free breakfast and baked goods. Taking a sip of coffee out of necessity, I grimaced at the taste. It was probably decent coffee, but I couldn't stand the stuff, having only started drinking it to get a jolt of energy after a night of drinking. I thought I'd still been drunk when she called.

"Liv, you're uh, looking a little...rough," she said slowly.

I glanced at my older sister Amanda from behind my coffee cup. The last time I had seen her, she'd had short blond hair styled into a pixie cut, but now her hair was past her shoulders and back to its original deep brown. Her eyes were the same color, and I guessed she had ditched the color contacts at some point.

Placing the coffee cup back on the table with shaky hands, I ran my fingers through my hair but got stuck in some knots and opted to tie it up in a messy bun instead. I sank into my oversized Carleton hoodie and looked down at my plaid pajama pants and flip flops. She might have a point.

"Gee, thanks, Amanda. Did you summon me here so early

just to insult my appearance?" I raised my eyebrows as she fidgeted with her coffee and took a deep breath.

"No, sorry, I didn't mean it like that. I'm just worried about you. I didn't ask you to meet me here to give you crap."

A cursory glance at my watch told me it was 7:15 a.m. *Lovely*. "So why did you then? I didn't even know you were back in town. Did the West Coast finally lose its appeal?" I was trying for a light teasing tone, but all that came through was bitterness. It was hard to mask my feelings so early in the morning.

She shook her head. "I moved back a couple of days ago. I'm staying with Mom and Dad," she practically whispered.

"*Moved?* I thought you were just visiting. Why would you move back? Isn't the West Coast some kind of promised land or something?"

She opened her mouth to answer but was interrupted by our waitress, Kelly, bringing our food to the table.

"Eggs, toast, hashbrowns, and bacon for you." She placed a large plate in front of my sister then turned to grab an even larger plate for me. "And pancakes, eggs, double meat, hash-browns, toast, with a side of extra sausage and a chocolate milk for you. Need anything else, ladies?"

We shook our heads and thanked her as she topped up our coffees and flashed a bright smile. Amanda eyed my food and I grinned mischievously. If she was gonna make me crawl out of bed at an ungodly hour, she was going to pay for it.

I took a big bite of pancake just as my sister bowed her head and closed her eyes for a moment. My fork froze in midair when I realized she was praying. My sister had been a lot of things over the years, but a praying woman wasn't one of them. Maybe I was still drunk.

She opened her eyes and loaded a bite of eggs on her fork, popping it into her mouth like nothing had happened. My fork was still suspended halfway between the plate and my mouth, and she cocked her head to the side questioningly. I shook my head to clear it and stabbed a breakfast sausage. After a few minutes of silence between us as we ate, she cleared her throat.

"So, how are you?" She eyed me over her coffee cup.

"Me? I'm fine," I answered as convincingly as I could. What G.G. had said the week before had really resonated with me, and I was doing my best to take her advice and look for the beauty in the path I was on. That had proven to be easier said than done, however, and I was still fumbling my way through a lot of rage.

"Really, Liv? You can talk to me you know. I'm your sister," she said gently.

I scoffed. "Amanda, I hardly know you. Sorry, I don't mean that. I just mean that we're not super close, ya know? I don't remember the last time we hung out like this. You have your life out west and that's fine, I'm happy for you. But let's not get all kumbaya on each other." I shoved another bite of pancake in my mouth to make myself shut up.

Instead of looking hurt, she nodded with understanding. "That's actually why I'm back," she started.

"Why?" I said with my mouth full.

She blew out a breath then said, "Because God told me to come back and fix my relationship with you."

I swallowed the enormous bite of food and it struggled down my throat scraping and stretching at every inch. Flailing for my chocolate milk, I guzzled it down to dislodge the crater the pancake had become. My eyes narrowed as I took a sip of coffee, trying to make it look casual when I felt anything but. I eyed her warily lest she do something else to catch me off guard. She looked normal enough in a cream cardigan and a ruffled skirt, still wearing her square-rimmed glasses—but, evidently, normal was relative.

"Since when do you care about God?" I mumbled.

"It's been a few months. It's weird, I know it's weird. I woke up one day with these boils all over my arms and legs and it freaked me out. The doctor gave me a prescription but instead of making it better, it got worse. Nothing they did helped, and I was getting really scared. It was so painful."

I'd never had anything like that happen to me before, and it sounded awful. Still, it didn't explain why she'd suddenly become…whatever she'd become.

She went on. "After a few weeks I got desperate. I reached out to a friend of mine who went to church and he didn't know what to do either. He offered to pray for me, and at first I said no. I didn't think it would do any good, you know? But then the pain reached an all-time high and I figured I had nothing to lose. He prayed, and overnight the pain reduced significantly."

That could have just been a coincidence, I thought to myself.

As if reading my mind, she said, "I figured it was a coincidence, but it was the only thing that had done any good in weeks, so I thought I'd try it out myself."

"What? Prayer?"

She looked at me sheepishly. "Yeah."

"Go on." I waved my hand to encourage her to finish the story so that I could go back to bed. A headache was brewing behind my eyes. No amount of free food was worth having to sit through a sermon, but she was my sister, so I'd placate her.

"I prayed and told God that if he was real, I'd need a sign. I wasn't just going to believe in some giant in the sky. When I woke up the next day, the boils had completely healed. There were just scabs left and those disappeared within a few days too."

"Wow," I murmured. It was impressive when someone believed in that kind of stuff, which I didn't.

"Right. Anyway, I started going to my friend's church and committed my life to Jesus, and then had a dream where He told me I needed to come back to Florida and fix our relationship so that you'd give Him a chance." She blew her breath out like she'd just finished a confession.

"Just like that?" I asked.

"Just like that. So here I am."

She stretched her hand across the table and I picked up the mug of coffee to keep mine out of reach.

"Okay, well, um, that's great, Amanda. Really. That sounds super cool…for you. It's not my thing but…you do you." I was rambling, and I knew it. My voice was also really high. What did one say to someone who had just told you they'd come to convert you to Christianity under the guise of a free breakfast?

"You're looking at me like I'm crazy." She pressed her lips together as if trying not to laugh.

The thought had crossed my mind. "No, no. I'm just not interested. I don't actually feel that well, so I think I'm just gonna head home and go back to bed. Thanks for breakfast, though." I gestured to my mostly untouched meal as I scrambled out of my seat to leave.

"Liv." Her tone stopped me in my tracks and I braced myself for what she was about to say. "I owe you a cookie," she said with a smile.

Standing outside, freshly baked cookies in hand, she pulled me into a hug and whispered in my ear, "I'll be praying for you to change your mind."

Don't hold your breath. "Okie dokie."

FINALLY, back in my bed, I pulled the covers right over my head to block out the world. My phone was set to silent but it rang, loud and shrill, alerting me that one of three people who were on emergency bypass was calling. I reached for it on my nightstand with my head still under the covers.

"Leah? You do know what time it is, right? I have the craziest story to tell you about my morning," I started.

"Liv." Her tone was flat, and I could tell that she'd been crying. I jolted up in bed.

"What's wrong?" I demanded.

After what felt like a million years she finally answered, "It's G.G."

And just like that, my world fell apart.

6

LUCAS

"I'm looking for Derek," I said to the first guy I saw in a hard hat.

He pointed out a man in work boots and a collared shirt standing in the middle of an unfinished house, about a hundred feet away. He looked up as I approached and excused himself from the conversation he was having with one of his crew members to walk over to me.

"Lucas?" he asked loudly above the sound of a saw.

"Yes, sir," I called back while extending my hand to shake his.

He was a good ten years older than I was, with dark hair just starting to show some gray. He had brown eyes and callouses on his hands, and held my application as he sized me up.

"You'll be the muscle," he said with a smirk.

"Whatever you need, sir."

I was sucking up and I knew it, but this was the sixth interview I'd had this week, and I was still without a job. The second they found out I'd just been released from prison, they thanked me for my time and backed away like I was about to throw them in the trunk of my beat-up car.

Derek looked at his watch. "You're early. I like that." He

nodded for me to follow him away from the noise. "This job is really physically demanding, but I think you'll be able to handle it. You don't have any previous experience in construction, but you seem eager enough to learn." He read through my application quickly. "What's with the two-year gap in work history? School or something?"

My shoulders slumped. It wasn't something I could lie about without risk of being terminated later if they found out. I blurted out, "I just got out of prison, but it wasn't for anything violent—and I hope you'll give me a chance anyway because I really want this job, and I'm willing to work my butt off for you." I trailed off, having said much more than I'd planned.

He looked me over again while I held my breath, waiting for his inevitable rejection. "You didn't hurt or kill anyone?" he asked with his head cocked to the side.

"No, sir. Nothing like that. I—"

He held up his hand to stop my confession. "I don't need to know your business, Lucas. What I need to know is if you're reliable and willing to show up every day."

I couldn't hide the surprise on my face. "Absolutely, I'll be here seven days a week if you need me to be." This hadn't happened with any of the other interviews, and I was still hesitant to let myself hope.

"We only work five days a week, but that's good to know. You'll need to pass a drug test. Is that going to be a problem?"

"Not at all." Despite myself, I could feel the hope rising. I could practically see my apartment already.

He nodded. "Okay, Lucas. I'll give you a shot. When can you start?"

I had to stop myself from shoving him and asking if he was serious. "I can start now if you want."

Derek chuckled. "That won't be necessary, but come by tomorrow and we'll get all your paperwork filled out. I'll start you at twenty-two dollars an hour, and we typically work a forty-hour work week. You got steel-toe boots?"

"No, but I could probably find some," I stammered. Maybe my brother had a pair lying around. With twenty-two dollars an hour, I'd be able to afford a pair of my own pretty quickly.

"Give your shoe and shirt size to Marco over there by the black truck and we'll have what you need tomorrow."

Before I could stop myself, I was saying, "I don't mean to press my luck or anything, but why are you giving me a chance?"

"I take it this isn't your first interview?" he asked with a laugh.

I grimaced. "Not exactly, no."

He paused for a moment before saying, "I'm a man of faith, Lucas, and I believe in second chances. Something in my gut is telling me to give you a shot, and I listen to those promptings like my life depends on them."

It wasn't at all what I was expecting him to say, but I was so grateful he could have told me the Easter Bunny had made him hire me and I still would have jumped for joy. "Well, thank you. Thank you so much. You won't regret this." I shook his hand with so much enthusiasm he practically had to wrench it free from my grip.

"I have a good feeling about you. Don't let me down." He moved back to the unfinished house, and I walked to my car in a daze after giving Marco my shoe and shirt sizes.

Had that really just happened?

A WEEK LATER, with an advance from Derek, I moved into a one-bedroom apartment in the same run-down building Adam, Isabel and Nori had lived in before they bought a house. The yellowed paint was cracked, the ceilings were covered in water stains, and fluorescent lights flickered in the hallway. There was no elevator, so Nate and I brought the second-hand couch I had bought at a thrift store up the stairs. I could have kissed every single stair, I was so happy to be out of my brother's place.

"Remind me again why you wouldn't just let my parents help you get a nicer place?" Nate huffed as he struggled under the weight of the couch.

"You know why."

If I was going to start over, I had to do it on my own. No more handouts. I knew he meant well, but his family had done so much for me in the past. It was time I landed on my own two feet.

We squeezed the couch through the door and put it against the wall. It was also going to serve as my bed until I could afford to buy one.

"Just so you know," Nate started, and I was already glaring at him because I knew that tone. "My mom is of the opinion that all the furniture in your room at their place is yours, so it's being delivered tomorrow. I tried to stop her." He flopped down on the couch.

"You tried to stop her, did you? And how exactly did she get my new address that only you and my boss have?"

"It's a mystery to me," he chortled.

I sank down beside him and punched him in the arm playfully. Some things never changed. Looking around the room, I started making a mental list of everything I wanted to do. Putting up some kind of curtains was at the top of my list, but since the building had a strict no-blanket-or-flag-as-curtains policy, they would have to wait until my next pay day. I had enough dishes and cutlery to last me a few meals before I had to wash them, and my windows overlooked a small courtyard with a tree growing in the middle.

All in all, I knew it wasn't much, but I also knew it was mine, and that was a huge first step.

7

OLIVIA

All the makeup in the world wasn't going to salvage my face from the blotches all over it. I had spent the entire week essentially inconsolable, mostly wailing into my pillow or stumbling around Indigo's office like a zombie until Carrie told me to go home. Giving myself one last look in the mirror, I smoothed out what I had donned as my funeral outfit—a black short-sleeve dress that hung down to my shins—and left the apartment to meet Mark and Leah outside.

Mark had insisted on driving me, and since I had asked Mela not to come out of fear that she wouldn't be able to stop herself from giving Ali a piece of her mind, it was either going with him or driving myself. I didn't think I'd be able to handle the Florida traffic in my mental state.

I slid into the back of Mark's black SUV. Leah was in the passenger seat and I gave her shoulder a squeeze.

"Thanks for picking me up, Mark." My voice sounded like I was a seventy-five-year-old chain smoker, and I winced when I heard it. I hadn't really spoken to anyone all week.

"Of course, Olivia. You're family." He gave me a smile through the rearview mirror and I couldn't bring myself to return it, so I looked out the window instead.

We both knew it wasn't exactly true. Technically I was nothing to him, but I supposed the fact that I was his daughter's sister made me family in his eyes. It was a sweet, albeit misplaced, sentiment.

Too soon we were pulling up to the funeral home and I watched as a line of people in black shuffled through the doors. Ali and Sheila stood off to the side receiving well wishes. I was surprised they were outside. It made me nervous because I hadn't really planned to talk to them.

Mark parked the SUV and Leah and I trailed behind him as he led the way. Just as we reached the doors, a woman in a large gaudy hat complete with feathers and ribbons pulled Mark and Leah aside to offer her condolences. Before I could decide if I was going in ahead of them or not, someone grabbed my arm and pulled me along. To my shock, the hand belonged to Ali.

She dragged me with impressive force while her mother Sheila pulled up the rear like in some kind of convoy. I realized as they cornered me into a private room and closed the door that the reason they'd been standing outside was for this exact purpose. The room was small and a tight fit. A large wooden desk sat to my left with a picture of a smiling family on it and a rolling chair tucked behind it. The walls were a dingy gray, reminding me of some kind of dungeon.

They each wore a long black dress so similar they could have been matching. Their green eyes were cold, and I hoped that mine were too because I didn't want them to get any satisfaction from upsetting me. Bracing myself for whatever speech they had prepared, I pulled out of Ali's grasp and folded my arms across my chest. Their eyes darted to each other then back to me as Sheila started the conversation.

"Olivia, we have some concerns about your presence here."

It felt like I had just fallen through a crack in the ice. My throat constricted and I found it difficult to take a deep breath. Everything felt cold; I started shivering. Were they seriously trying to stop me from attending G.G.'s funeral?

"Wh-what?" I stammered.

"It's not that you're not welcome," Sheila said as if talking to a child. "It's just that there are a lot of our family members here and they don't know about you. It might get confusing." Her hand was touching my arm in a way that would normally be soothing, but it felt more like she was trying to keep me from leaving the room than comforting me.

"Okay..." I was numb and entirely unclear about what they were asking of me. I did, however, notice how Sheila had said "our" family, meaning hers and Ali's. Not mine. *Never mine.*

Ali seemed to sense my confusion and stepped in. "We don't want anyone knowing that you're related to us," she said bluntly.

I sucked in a breath. *This* was what they were worried about? "What do you think I'm going to do exactly? Rip the mic from the minister and make an announcement?" I nearly laughed out loud. It was a ridiculous thought, and yet they were eyeing each other nervously as if that was precisely what they believed I'd do. "That's it, isn't it? You think I'm going to use G.G.'s funeral as a way to let everyone know that I'm related to you." I moved for the door.

"This isn't the time or place for an announcement like that, Olivia," Ali called after me with a warning behind her words.

I whipped around. "You know what? You're right, Ali. This isn't the time. The time was almost twenty-three years ago when I was born. The fact that the two of you would even think I'd do something so...so..." I couldn't even think of the right word, I was so pissed. The thought of hijacking G.G.'s funeral had never occurred to me.

Suddenly Mark burst through the door. He took in the scene before him and his usually calm eyes flashed with rage. "Unbelievable. The two of you are unbelievable. I knew you'd do something, but I'd hoped I was wrong." He pointed at them and seemed to take a menacing step, which caused them to back up against the wall. As he stepped in front of me, I understood that he was merely providing an exit for me, which I didn't hesitate to take.

Leah stood on the other side of the door with wide eyes, squeezing the life out of her small purse. "I've never seen my dad so angry," she whispered.

I linked my arm through hers and moved us into the main room, where the funeral would soon be starting. Rows of benches lined either side of the room, and I figured that Leah and Mark would be sitting in the front row, but I knew that Ali would lose her mind if I sat with them. I slid into the back bench.

Leah shook her head adamantly. "My dad said you're sitting with us."

"Leah, your mom will flip out. It's easier this way." I sighed.

"You're sitting with us," she repeated, leaving no room for discussion, and then held my hand and practically dragged me up to the front. I could see where she got her determination, having just been accosted by Ali.

A few minutes later, Mark flopped down next to Leah, looking thoroughly exhausted. Sheila and Ali made their way to the front and sat in the bench row across from us without so much as a glance in our direction. Their solemn expressions mirrored each other, and I did my best to remind myself that they had just lost their loved one too. My eyes were trained on the slide show projected on a large screen at the front of the room. It was cycling through pictures of G.G. from infancy to adulthood.

One picture stood out to me and my eyes narrowed as I took a closer look the second time it came around. G.G. was alone in the picture and grinning like she was on top of the world. As my gaze zeroed in on her hand, my suspicions were confirmed. They had tried to cut me out of the picture, but there was my hand, resting on top of hers. I pressed my lips together and did my best not to think about it. The original sat framed on my dresser and they could never take that away from me.

The minister, wearing a black suit, walked up to the small stage to begin the service. What followed was an entire funeral designed for someone who looked a lot like G.G. but certainly wasn't her. They talked about her as though she was a stuffy stranger who enjoyed seafood and living in a care facility. I wondered if they knew her at all. The only seafood she liked was shrimp. And where was Matteo? I hadn't seen him anywhere.

The service ended and we stood up to leave, the front rows emptying first. I walked down the aisle avoiding eye contact with anyone, lest they somehow discovered the family resemblance, and caught a glance of Matteo in the second-to-last row. I stepped over to him immediately.

"What are you doing back here?" I demanded.

He shrugged and said, "Ruth's family thought it would be best for me to stay out of the photo." He smiled apologetically. Out of the photo? I replayed his words in my head as the rest of the room began filing out quietly.

"Do you mean out of the *picture*?" I hissed.

"Yes, yes, that's it. Sorry, *tesoro,* I sometimes don't have the right words." He patted my arm and waited for me to let him by.

This isn't the time for a scene. I reminded myself of that over and over again as I walked arm in arm with Matteo into the reception area. It was absolutely packed, and people were still giving their condolences to the rest of the family in some kind of receiving line. I wouldn't be welcome there, so I walked around the room eyeing the outrageous amount of food spread out over several serving tables. There were smaller tables and chairs for the guests to sit and socialize at. What really caught my eye was the table with about a hundred glasses of champagne. I sauntered over and downed one immediately while double-fisting two more as I casually walked away.

Twenty minutes later I was on my fifth drink and staring daggers at Sheila and Ali from across the room. *How dare they try to stop me from attending my own great-grandmother's funeral. I was closer to her than they ever were. And where do they get off keeping Matteo out of the photo…* Sheila leaned over to whisper something in Ali's ear, their eyes never leaving mine.

Maybe I should cause a scene. It was only what they'd deserve. All their little secrets poured out like this glass of champagne. I lifted said glass to my lips to take a sip, but it was empty. When had that happened? I moved to get another glass, all the while continuing to glare at Ali and Sheila. Why should they decide who got to sit at the front anyway? Maybe there was a mic around here somewhere. I started to look around when someone blocked my view.

"Liv?" Leah was staring at me with a concerned look on her face. Or faces. There seemed to be more than one of her. As I tried to focus, she kept talking. "Are you okay? I know what my mom did was messed up, but you look like you're debating picking a fight with her."

"How'd you know?" I laughed. Or at least that's what I had meant to do but it came out more like a snort. I snatched another glass of champagne from the table and some of it sloshed over the side and fell to the floor.

"Maybe that's not such a good idea," Leah said eyeing the drink in my hand.

I looked into her worried eyes and it took a while for the fog to clear from my thoughts—but once it did, I realized how much I was upsetting her. "Crap, I'm sorry, Leah. I should go." My words sounded slurred in my ears. Placing the glass back on the table, I pulled out my phone and—with difficulty, since I could hardly make out the screen—ordered an Uber to come pick me up.

"You don't have to leave," Leah said softly but her tone indicated that it might be better if I did. She wasn't wrong.

G.G. wouldn't have been happy to see me drowning my sorrows with champagne. She also wouldn't have been happy with her funeral as a whole, but my feelings on the matter were inconsequential. Still, I didn't want to upset my sister—or G.G., wherever she was.

"S'okay, Leah. I'll call you later." I pulled her much closer than was probably necessary and said, "Make sure they aren't rude to Matteo. She wouldn't have wanted that." Brushing the tears from my cheeks, I left before I could make a bigger spectacle of myself.

8

LUCAS

The day of the engagement party had finally arrived, and I was still woefully unprepared to face Liv. I'd been looking forward to this day with equal parts longing and dread. Part of me still had my exit strategy carefully in place, but a bigger part knew that the second I laid eyes on her, there was no way I'd be able to leave without speaking to her.

Fumbling with the buttons on the dress shirt I had planned to wear, I opted instead for a plain white t-shirt over black dress pants. I spent entirely too long trying to tame my hair into something that looked presentable. Eventually I'd get a haircut when I had some extra cash.

I was a few weeks into my job, and it had been going well. The work was physically demanding, but it felt great to get my hands dirty and be out in the sun all day. I didn't think I'd ever been this tanned before. Plus, my boss, Derek, was great. He wasn't the preachy kind of Christian I was familiar with. He was just a nice guy who treated everyone with respect—even if they had a criminal record.

I took one last look in the bathroom mirror and grabbed my keys. A few minutes later I was pulling into Nate's parents' club where the party was being held. Sheepishly I handed my keys to the valet parking attendant and winced as he pulled away, leaving a cloud of smoke in my car's wake. I'd get around to fixing that sometime.

Nate had warned me that Liv would likely already be there and Mela would be with her. I was to be on the lookout for them so Mela didn't have the chance to club me over the head with a bottle of champagne. Though he'd said it with a laugh, I still wasn't entirely sure he was kidding.

By the time I'd mustered up the nerve to get there, the party was in full swing. Walking in, I felt like I had a target on my back and kept an eye open for a floating bottle of alcohol positioned over my head.

There were a lot of people at the party, and I didn't recognize most of them. It was loud in a way I wasn't used to and my senses felt like they were overloading. Many people talked animatedly with their hands, and I figured they were part of Mela's Italian family. It also explained the volume level. I made my way through the crowd to the bar and ordered a Coke, which I planned to nurse until after I had seen Liv. I needed to keep a level head, and alcohol would only hinder that.

Leaning against the bar, I surveyed the crowd. Everyone seemed to be having a great time, which Nate would be happy about. Big parties weren't the scene for either of us, but he'd gotten used to being around them over the years of dating Mela. The giant white and gold banner with 'CONGRATULATIONS NATHANIEL & CARMELLA' on it caught my eye, and then I froze in place as my gaze fell upon Liv standing directly under it.

Seeing her there, for a moment I forgot to breathe, and then all the air left my lungs like someone had sucker-punched me. She was as beautiful as ever, if not more so now, and I wanted to rush to her like I would on a football field, shoving everyone out of my way. I didn't.

She was wearing a green dress and her hair was longer than it had been the last time I'd seen her. After all this time apart, I was tempted to throw myself at her feet and beg for her forgiveness, but I stopped myself, knowing it was the last thing I deserved.

As she smiled at Mela, the thought of her smile fading once she caught sight of me made me hesitate even more. I wasn't ready for this. It had been a mistake to come even if I'd convinced myself it was for Nate. Liv's head swung in my direction and I ducked to lose myself in the crowd before either she or Mela could see me.

I needed a minute—or ten—to calm my nerves. The now warm glass of Coke I was holding started to slip out of my grip as my sweaty palm struggled to keep it in my hand. My eyes scanned the party as fast as humanly possible, looking for an abandoned corner where I could regain my composure. Not finding a quiet place in the room, I spotted Nate's parents and made a split-second decision to head over to them.

"Lucas!" Mrs. Martin pulled me into a hug the moment I was within reach. Mr. Martin flashed a grin at me and punched my shoulder playfully.

"Mr. and Mrs. Martin, it's so good to see you," I stammered. My voice was shaking, but the party was loud and I doubted they'd heard it.

"Nick and Nancy," Mrs. Martin corrected me.

I'd never given in to calling them by their first names. It just felt too weird, so I nodded politely.

"Thank you for the furniture. It was entirely too generous."

"Lucas, you're practically family. We're always happy to help," she murmured.

"Have you been working out? You look like some kind of bouncer at a club." Mr. Martin squinted at me like it would help him make sense of my size.

For some reason this felt hilarious, and I threw back my head to laugh as though the mere act could lighten the heaviness within me. "Yeah, I've been working out more lately," I replied while my eyes continued to dart towards where Liv stood with Mela and now Nate.

We chatted for a couple more minutes, and it helped me feel much calmer than when I'd first walked over. It was great to see them both, even if I was distracted.

I could feel it the moment Liv realized I was there. Out of the corner of my eye I saw her jaw drop, and the heat of her gaze started burning a hole in my chest.

Mrs. Martin leaned over and whispered into my ear, "Good luck, Lucas. I'm rooting for you two." Before giving me a little shove towards Liv.

I took a deep, steadying breath, and then I started towards her.

9

OLIVIA

"C*hampagne?"* A waiter in black pants and a crisp white button-up shirt leaned his tray towards me. I shook my head quickly.

"No, thank you." After G.G.'s funeral, the alcohol I had gorged on had made a second appearance in my toilet, and I wasn't keen on revisiting that experience.

It had been three weeks since the funeral, but her loss was still fresh in my mind. It broke my heart that I hadn't had the chance to say goodbye to her. That I'd never play cards with her again. That my Tuesday nights were to be spent drinking or clubbing or doing whatever I could to forget I should instead be playing cards with her.

I smoothed down the turquoise dress Mela had insisted I wear to her engagement party and re-secured the wristlet holding my phone and lip gloss on my right hand.

The room was sparkling under a thousand lights strung across the ceiling. Standing tables draped with cream-colored tablecloths were placed strategically for guests to put their drinks on while they mingled. Servers with trays of drinks and food moved through the crowd. Black and gold streamers hung from the lights, and matching foil balloon bouquets with "Congratulations" written on them were tethered to the ground every few feet, and swayed gently back and forth as people walked by. There had to be at least a hundred people in the room to celebrate Nate and Mela. It was a lovely party, and I was doing everything I could to cheer myself up.

I stood out of the way under a giant banner congratulating the engaged couple. I noticed Mela walking towards me and plastered a smile on my face so as not to ruin her party.

"You don't have to do that," she said in a singsong voice.

"Do what?" I replied in the same way.

"Pretend like your heart isn't broken over the loss of G.G. I told you that if you needed to sit this out you could."

"I know. But I'm your maid of honor. How would it have looked if I skipped out on your engagement party?" I mumbled the words into my glass of water.

"Since when do we care about stuff like that, Liv? You're my best friend, and if you need to go, Nate and I will understand." She put her hand on my arm and gave it a gentle squeeze.

My eyes filled with tears, and I looked up at the ceiling, willing them not to fall. When I was sure the moment had passed, I smiled at her. "Maybe being around all these loud happy people is exactly what I need."

Nate sauntered over, giving Mela a look that would have melted even the iciest of hearts. Not that I could blame him. The dress she was wearing was a delicate swirl of soft blush tulle that shimmered under the glow of the lights. Intricate lace bloomed across the fitted bodice and the skirt flared out in layered waves that caught the air with each movement making her look like she was floating instead of walking.

I couldn't help but feel slightly envious of their love story. There were no complications or disappearing acts. They were in love and pretty much always had been. Maybe I'd have that someday.

Suddenly Mela gripped my arms painfully and turned me

towards her. The look of panic on her face sent my heart racing. "Oh my God. Liv, I swear I didn't know."

I looked around for the danger. "Didn't know what?"

Her eyes darted to the crowd, and she motioned with her head for me to turn and look at whatever had her so freaked out. Bracing myself, I slowly turned and, at first, I didn't see anything out of the ordinary. A tall, rather muscular man stood chatting with Nate's parents across the room. My eyes continued scanning the crowd, and I was just about to ask Mela what she was so upset about when the drink I was holding dropped to the ground, spilling its contents everywhere.

It was as if my body had responded before my mind could catch up. The way the man speaking to Nate's parents tilted his head... I had seen it a hundred times, and at that moment I realized that they weren't just talking to some random man; they were talking to *Lucas*. I gasped.

There he stood, his new muscles making him nearly unrecognizable, and yet his mannerisms were still familiar to me. He seemed much taller than he had been, as though he'd had some bizarre growth spurt over the last few years. Didn't that stop in your teens? He'd be twenty-three now.

Conflicting thoughts competed for my attention, and I stood frozen in place as I wondered where he'd been all this time.

I studied him as he continued talking to Nick and Nancy—who looked delighted to have their prodigal son back—and felt almost jealous that it seemed so easy for them to welcome him with open arms. I had finally gotten used to the idea of him being gone and now here he was. It was confusing, like I was waking up from a dream.

The moment he turned and his eyes locked on mine, my breath hitched and my legs turned to mush, nearly causing me to drop to the floor. Though Nate and Mela were still standing with me, I was hardly aware of them. I looked away from Lucas's hopeful expression and tried to find somewhere I could escape to. There were too many people at the party and the room felt like it was closing in on me.

My feet seemed to be moving involuntarily as they brought me closer to him. In the same way, he moved to me like invisible magnets were pulling us together. His measured gaze never left mine, and the closer he got, the more clearly I could see the determination in his bright hazel eyes. Looking at him was painful. It reminded me in equal parts how much I'd loved him and how badly he'd hurt me. It was confusing to say the least.

"...and you thought our engagement party was the right time and place for Lucas to ambush my best friend?" Mela was fuming beside me, having apparently come along while I walked to Lucas.

"I thought it was a good idea," Nate said with a shrug.

"You thought it was such a great idea that you kept it from me? Obviously, you knew I'd never be okay with *this*." She pointed at Lucas as she said it.

Mela continued to berate him but all I could focus on was the boy—scratch that, the man—who was now standing in front of me.

"Hey, Liv," Lucas murmured. I watched as he ran his hand through his hair, knowing that he only did that when he was nervous. I couldn't help but feel a small sense of satisfaction, assuming that he was likely as flustered as I was.

"Lucas." My tone was frosty, and he winced. Guilt churned in my stomach, but I ignored it.

"How have you been?" he tried again.

"Fine, thank you. And yourself?"

Mela trembled with anger beside me while I used formality as a shield against him.

"I've been...okay."

He chose his words carefully. I could see there was a lot he wasn't saying. I wanted to ask him where he'd been. Why he'd never come back for me even after I'd told him I loved him in that letter. But instead, I forced my eyes to go cold and took a step back.

"If you'll excuse me." I turned and practically ran to the side door that led out to the club's garden. Once I was alone, I gasped for breath while wrapping my arms around myself as tightly as I could. *Keep it together, Liv.* As much as I didn't want to fall apart, I couldn't help it. I had loved this man for years and mourned his loss over and over. All I'd wanted was for him to come back, and now that he had, there seemed to be an impenetrable wall between us.

My breath was coming out in ragged gasps sounding unnatural in my ears. I sat down on the bench nearby to try to calm myself. I forced myself to stay still in case anyone was watching. As soon as I regained my composure, I'd leave. Then I'd never have to see Lucas O'Connell again.

10

LUCAS

I watched as Liv walked out the side door and moved to follow her, but my path was blocked by a ball of Italian rage in the form of Mela. She grabbed my arm and held me in place with such a strong grip that even Nate went pale.

"What did you think, Lucas? That you could just swoop in here after your little disappearing act and all would be forgiven?" She pushed a finger into my chest and went on. "Don't hold your breath. You ruined any chance of reconciliation when you deserted her."

"Mel—" Nate started, but she whipped around to face him.

"You and I will have words about this later when we aren't hosting over a hundred people as the 'happy couple'." She laughed loudly while some of their guests walked by us and then narrowed her eyes, digging her finger deeper into my chest. "Don't think this is over, Lucas. I have ways to make it seem like an accident."

She smoothed out my shirt, beamed up at me, and dragged Nate away while he looked at her with a mixture of fear and desire. She was downright terrifying.

Before Mela could have some of her cousins throw me in the trunk of a car, I hurried over to the door through which Liv had left. It opened into a private garden with colorful flowers I didn't even know.

In the middle of it all was a fountain lit up by submersible lighting which I only recognized because we had installed some at a job site the week before. There, on the other side of the fountain, Liv sat on a bench.

I walked around the circular cobblestone path slowly until I reached her. She sat with her head in her hands, breathing too fast.

"Liv?" I asked hesitantly.

"Go away, Lucas," she cried through ragged breathing.

"Not until your breathing slows down, okay? Then I swear I'll leave. I could go get Mela for you?" I offered, though it was the last thing I wanted to do.

"No. Don't get Mela."

I sat down on the bench beside her giving her space. She breathed in through her nose and out through her mouth rhythmically as she tried to get a hold of herself.

After a couple of minutes, she drew herself up and looked at me warily. I couldn't blame her, but it stung all the same.

"You okay?" I made myself keep my hands on my lap.

"Sure," she said eventually. Her tone was biting, and it seemed like the only answer I was going to get.

"How have you been?"

She moved away slightly as if suddenly needing more space between us.

"How have I been? Really Lucas?" she said, and I saw her fists clenching and unclenching.

"I'm sorry, I honestly don't know what to say right now."

She studied me for a moment. "Where have you been?"

A slow, creeping tension settled in my ribs, making it feel like I was sucking my breath through a straw. I couldn't tell her the truth, she'd never understand. "I've been on an…extended leave."

Her shoulders drooped and her eyes seemed glassy, as if she'd been trying not to cry.

"You seem sad, Liv," I said.

She laughed but sounded bitter. "My feelings stopped being your business a long time ago."

Liv was right, but I hated that fact all the same. "I'm sorry."

She stood up quickly and faced me. "I don't want your apologies, I want answers. Where have you been, and why didn't you come back?"

I had in fact come back, but I didn't think pointing it out would go over particularly well. Her fingernails were digging into her palms, and it made my chest ache to see it.

My hand reached for hers and I gently pried her fingernails out of her skin. "You only dig your nails into your palms when you're really stressed out." I rubbed her palms softly, attempting to erase the little crescents marking them. Touching her again made my heart race.

"Lucas," she warned, but didn't pull her hands away.

"I know that it's been a long time, Liv. But I still know you."

Gently she pulled her hands out of mine. The emptiness felt uncomfortable, and I shoved my hands in my pockets to distract from it. There was less than a foot between us, but we might as well have been miles apart. The silence stretched on and I felt like a bigger jerk with each passing second.

A gentle breeze rustled through her hair and the scent of her shampoo brought me memories of holding her in my arms and nuzzling her neck while we talked late into the night. I thought I had missed her, but now that I was sitting here, I realized that it was more than that. A whole part of me had been missing these past few years, and here it was, just out of reach.

I moved to my knees in front of her placing my hands on her legs. "Liv, I'm so sorry." My voice cracked on the last word and I cleared my throat to regain my composure. "I've regretted leaving you every single day. I don't think I'll ever stop. There are…things…that kept us apart. That kept me away from you."

"Things? Like what? Don't you think I deserve a better explanation than that?" She folded her arms across her chest and shivered like she was cold, despite the warmth of the evening.

I stood up as I spoke. "Yes, of course you do."

"That's it?" She laughed.

"Look, I was away but now I'm back. I thought that…" I made a movement towards her and she recoiled, which stopped me in my tracks.

"You thought what? It's not water under the bridge, Lucas. You're a real piece of work, you know that? And honestly, I've moved on." She held my gaze as she delivered the blow.

The words cut me deeper than I'd expected. Her moving on was exactly what I deserved, but it still pained me to think about her with someone else. I'd been an idiot hoping she would welcome me back with open arms.

"Right, yeah. Of course," I said, trying to sound casual. It might have worked if it weren't for the strain in my voice. "I figured you wouldn't just wait around." *Liar.* "I really am sorry, Liv." The smile I attempted felt foreign on my face. Something was lodged in my throat and it wouldn't move, no matter how many times I swallowed.

Her eyes softened for a moment and I thought I saw a flash of guilt cross her face, but it was gone so fast I wasn't sure. "I couldn't spend my life pining for a ghost, Lucas." She surprised me by choking on a sob. Without looking back, she walked out of the garden through a gate I hadn't noticed before.

I wanted to chase her and tell her everything while begging for forgiveness. But I knew it wouldn't help. She'd never understand. She was too good for me, and I'd always known it. The best thing I could do for her was let her go.

So I stood still, forcing myself to stay rooted in place as she walked out of my life again.

11

OLIVIA

"This is...quaint," my sister said softly.

"Quaint?" I repeated as though I'd misheard her.

"Yeah, you know? Eccentric, unique, attractively unusual?" she said as her lips quivered, hiding a smile.

I didn't know why I had come. Still reeling from the engagement party the week before, I had wanted to say no to coffee with Amanda, but I'd had no real reason to. We were at a cozy little cafe in a beach town a few counties over. I stared off into space my mind drifting as I thought about all that had transpired over the past few weeks.

"Earth to Liv." My sister waved her hand in front of my face, snapping me back to the present.

"Sorry." I pulled my tea bag out of my cup and placed it on the saucer beside it. It was delicious, as most London Fogs were, but I was so distracted that it was hard to enjoy. I chided myself for that internally. Here I was, sitting at a beachside café, watching the ocean waves lap against the sand—and I wasn't even enjoying it.

"I was really sorry to hear about G.G.," my sister said.

"Were you?" My tone was surprised and my sister clicked her tongue. "I didn't mean it like *that*, Amanda."

"How *did* you mean it?" She cocked her head to the side, looking as though she was genuinely trying to understand me.

"All I meant was that Mom and Dad weren't exactly thrilled that I had such a close relationship with her after the whole Jason drama, so I thought maybe you felt the same way. I was never trying to replace you guys."

"Of course you weren't," she said with a laugh, as though the mere idea was preposterous. "I, for one, am entirely irreplaceable." Laughter danced behind her dark eyes, and I felt my mouth twitch upwards involuntarily. She reached over the table and gently touched my hand. "Will you tell me about her?"

I swallowed hard and nodded. "She was the best. Mischievous, competitive, hilarious…" I paused, remembering the way G.G. had begged forgiveness for not stepping in to help when I was born. "She was kind and compassionate. And she gave the best hugs." Blinking back tears, I brought my mug to my lips and took a sip.

"She sounds wonderful. I'm sorry I never got the chance to meet her." Amanda squeezed my hand and took a long drink of her coffee. We watched the sea for a few minutes, lost in thought. "I'm sure God has a plan. He always does; even in death."

Anger ripped through me. "Are you kidding me right now?" I demanded.

Her eyes widened with surprise. "Liv, I didn't mean anything by it," she said holding her hands up in defense.

"Is that supposed to make me feel better? Some dude in the sky had a plan and that's why he took G.G.? Save it, Amanda. I'm not interested in sentimental drivel or platitudes about a fictional God's plans for our lives." I practically spat the words at her, drawing a look of concern from a lady at a table nearby.

"I'm sorry, Liv. That was really insensitive of me." She looked at me with such sadness that it was almost laughable. Knowing we had a thirty-minute drive back together, I opted to let it go.

"Forget about it."

After a few more minutes of introspection, she spoke again. "Can I ask you something?"

If this had anything to do with God I was going to lose it.

"It has nothing to do with God," she said, reading my mind.

"Sure." I motioned for her to ask.

"What happened with Mom and Dad? They're surprisingly tightlipped about the whole thing, but I know something big must have gone down," she said with curiosity burning behind her eyes.

I looked back out at the waves as though drawing strength from the ocean. "It started a long time ago when I found Jason. But it got much worse during the court case against Chris."

She nodded with understanding, and I was sure she remembered that whole ordeal. Older psychotic ex-boyfriend tried to rape me and threatened to put Lucas in jail unless I got back with him, resulting in a court case years later with several other victims. He was still doing time and would be for several more years.

"I remember the court case. Mom was acting like she had something stuck up her…well, let's just say she was worse than usual." Amanda grimaced, and it reminded me that she hadn't had an easy relationship with our parents either. It helped me relax.

"Right. So, when she found out that I hadn't turned Chris in because I didn't want Lucas to go to prison, she flipped out. She accused me of allowing terrible things to happen to other girls so that I could protect a boy."

"That's completely unfair," Amanda said, her nostrils flaring as she drew an angry breath.

It felt nice to have someone in my family on my side for once. "Yeah, it was rough. After that, things were pretty frosty between us, but the final break in our relationship—at least with Mom—was when I shattered my ankle."

"What happened?" she asked, seeming to brace herself for what I was about to say.

"I got a little...depressed..." I trailed off. Depressed didn't even begin to cover it. It had been like being shrouded in darkness every hour of every day. As if all the hope in the world had disappeared and in its wake had come a bone-chilling, everlasting emptiness.

Amanda stayed quiet, sensing I needed a minute to come back to the present.

"Anyway," I went on. "Mom was sympathetic in the very beginning but grew tired of my 'feelings' quickly. She started telling me to just get over it like I was milking my depression. Even after I got a clinical diagnosis, she was still adamant that I needed to just be happy already."

I shook my head at the memory while Amanda pressed her lips together; perhaps she was trying hard not to say something she wouldn't be able to take back.

"When I was in the darkest part of the journey, she started demanding early repayment of a loan I owed them."

"Why early?" Amanda asked.

"I think she figured it would force me to get a job and therefore I'd magically be happy again."

"Did it work?" Her expression indicated that she already knew the answer.

"No. No, it didn't. What it did do, though, was make me realize that I could never count on her. She's not reliable when the chips are down, you know? But Jason...he was. He hooked me up with my job at Indigo through an acquaintance of his and gave me enough money to move out, even refusing to let me pay him back. He really showed up for me."

My eyes misted as I thought about my biological dad. Like a tree in a raging storm, his presence had been strong and rooted. I could count on him, and that had really solidified our bond.

"What about Dad? Actually, let me guess. He was sympathetic but took Mom's side, right?"

"Yeah, that about sums it up."

"I'm sorry, Liv. I should have been there for you. I was so

caught up in my own life and my own problems that I left everything behind; including you. Can you ever forgive me?" Her eyes welled up.

I thought about the way that her and my brothers had left the East Coast and never seemed to look back. It had hurt to think I was some forgotten piece of her past. Yet here she was, trying to make amends. She had come back, and that counted for something.

"Of course, Amanda. Don't even worry about it." To be honest, it felt good to have another ally.

12

LUCAS

I couldn't get Liv out of my head. Ever since I'd seen her at the engagement party the week before, she was never far from my thoughts. All I wanted was a chance to make things right, but I was pretty sure I had screwed things up to the irredeemable point.

"You good, Lucas? You seem restless today." Derek eyed me as I dug out the path for the walkway we'd be laying.

"Yeah, yeah, I'm fine. Just have some nervous energy I guess," I said, realizing that I had been bouncing on my toes for a while.

The job site we'd been at for a few weeks was finally close to completion. The house had been framed up and drywalled, a pool had been installed with submersible lighting, a brand-new lawn had been laid with fresh sod, new trees, bushes, and flowers planted, and now we were going to build an interlock walkway to complete the look. I had to admit, it felt good to be a part of making it all come together.

Derek grabbed a shovel and joined me. He was a solid boss that way, not afraid to get his hands dirty and help when needed. His company, J.C. Enterprises, had multiple crews running several job sites simultaneously. They did everything from building houses to paving driveways.

We worked in companionable silence for a few minutes with the shovel splitting the earth and our grunts as the only sound while we hauled the dirt into a pile.

"How did you start your company?" I surprised myself by asking him. I wasn't normally the prying kind.

"It's a pretty cool story, actually." He wiped his face with the bottom of his shirt. "My dad left us when I was a kid, so my mom raised me on her own with social assistance. Growing up poor wasn't easy, especially since my mom wanted me to have the same opportunities that any other kid had, so she moved us to just within the boundary of a fancy arts school that had to accept me because I lived there. I was the smelly kid with dirty clothes because we didn't have a washing machine."

I grimaced as I hit a rock with my shovel. *Why is he telling me his life story? And why does it sound so much like mine?*

"I got sick of being *that* kid, so I started stealing nicer clothes, shoes, jewelry, and then I moved on to televisions to know what shows everyone was talking about. And then it escalated to ATVs so I could have fun on the weekends, which eventually led to me getting into stealing cars for a guy who would send them overseas on shipping containers."

Now I'd stopped shoveling and was openly staring at him. There was no way this clean cut, nice-to-everyone, goody-two-shoes had been acting out Grand Theft Auto as a teenager.

"I made a lot of money," he continued, "and finally felt like I was making something of myself. And then I got pinched stealing the wrong car at the wrong time, and they tried to pin the entire operation on me."

He took a long pull of his water, and I did the same with mine.

"The feds wanted me to roll over on the guys who were actually running it, but I wasn't about to be a rat. I knew they didn't have enough evidence to prove that some eighteen-year-old kid had orchestrated an elaborate scheme to steal cars and sell them overseas, and I was right. I got a six-year sentence and got out in five on good behavior."

"You went to prison?" We were laying down a type of filter cloth to prevent weeds from growing up and through the bricks.

"What, you think you're the only one who's gone to prison?" His laugh had an edge to it.

I'd spent two years there, and that was enough to make me never want to go back. I couldn't imagine being in jail for five.

"You just seem…not like a criminal?" I winced at my poor choice of words as we started filling the hole we'd dug with gravel. He nodded like he understood what I meant, and I was grateful not to have to explain.

"While I was in prison, there was a pastor who came to encourage the inmates every week. I ignored him for the first two years, was openly hostile to him for the next year, and then I shocked the hell out of us both when I asked him how to become a Christian."

I kept quiet and waited for him to continue.

"After that, we started meeting regularly to help me figure out what I was going to do when I got out. So many people end up back in prison because they fall right back into their old habits. It's hard to get hired, as you well know, and so they just return to their life of crime hoping that they won't get caught the next time. I didn't want that to be my story."

"Yeah, I can understand that." It would have been easier to go back to stealing than it had been to get a job, but I was never going back to prison. "So then, what happened?" I tried to sound chill, but the truth was that I was hanging on to every word even as we compacted the gravel with a machine and he had to yell over the noise to be heard.

He smiled at me knowingly. "I started learning everything I could about business and reading plans and managing people. Growing up in a hole in the wall with roaches and rats made me want to be a part of building safe homes for people. When I got out, the pastor I'd been meeting with got me a job with one of his congregants, who ran a construction company. I worked for him until I was his right-hand man and then he gave me a loan to start J.C. Enterprises. The rest is history."

"Your boss gave you a loan to start a competing company?" I shook my head in disbelief. That made no sense. Who would do that?

"He loved Jesus." He shrugged like that was explanation enough.

We shoveled stone dust on top of the compacted gravel, and Derek began to carefully grade a section to get it ready for laying the bricks. We'd been talking for two hours, and it had felt like five minutes.

"I grew up without a dad too," I said quietly. The words were out of my mouth before I even realized I was saying them. He gave me a sad kind of smile and stayed quiet while I went on. "He left when I was three, and my mom didn't really cope all that well to single life with three boys."

"Oof, three boys are a lot to handle."

"We were. My brothers were in and out of jail a bunch, and I didn't want that to be my life. I met a girl, fell in love, and then we broke up. My dad came looking for me, and I was excited. I'd been living with my best friend's family, and I thought that maybe we'd make our own family again, just me and him. But then he started asking me for money, and when I told him I didn't have any, he confessed that he'd only come because he found out I was living with my rich friend and thought I'd be able to help him."

Why was I telling him all this? Maybe it was easier because he was practically a stranger and we had some pretty big things in common. And maybe he was a little like the dad I'd never had.

"That's rough, Lucas. I'm sorry to hear that. Sometimes men just aren't capable of growing up. You deserved better than that."

I shrugged. Did I? Who knew? "Is that why you gave me a chance?"

"Is what why?" He looked confused.

"Because I have a record, like you." The last thing I wanted was to be someone's charity case.

"I gave you a chance because God told me to. And I know that probably sounds nuts, but it's the truth. He sent that pastor to me in prison and then orchestrated a job for me on the outside. I do the same for others when I can. I've always been grateful to those men, and now I go to the prison I was incarcerated at and encourage the inmates there the way my pastor did for me."

"You go back there? Voluntarily?" I was incredulous. It wasn't something I'd ever do myself.

"Of course. Look, we're more than the bad choices we've made, but when you're locked up that feels like a pipe dream for someone else. I know how it is to sit in a cell and wonder if that's all you'll ever be. I needed that pastor to give me hope when I had none, and it's my privilege to do the same for others. Maybe you can come with me some time," he suggested.

I bit back the laugh that nearly flew out of my mouth. *Fat chance.* "Yeah, maybe," I said evasively.

"Get back to work, slacker," he said with a laugh, as if he knew full well I'd never go.

We finished the walkway, nailed some nap edge in to keep it together, and then filled the cracks with polymeric sand to seal it. As I lightly misted the brick with a hose to activate the sand, I thought about what Derek had said. It didn't feel like I was more than the bad choices I had made, but maybe, just maybe, he wasn't totally full of crap.

13

OLIVIA

I walked up the steps to Nate and Mela's townhouse. It had been a gift from his parents, supposedly for when he turned twenty-five. Yet, after the death of Mela's mom and considering that they were clearly going to get married, they'd given it to them early.

The sun was shining brightly as I waited for Mela to let me in, so I stood in the shade of their small porch. A few billowy clouds dotted the sky; as it was the last week of October, a bit of a chill was in the air, but nothing compared to the cold in New York around this time. I thought of the way the trees would be changing colors there and longed to return.

A couple of cute pumpkins sat at the edge of the step, and I smiled at Mela's attempt to be festive.

The door swung open and she stood there in a satin robe with her wet hair wrapped up in a white towel. Her brown eyes had a bit of a wild look as they darted back and forth like she was expecting to be attacked.

"Uh, you okay? You were expecting me, right?" I said as I held back my laughter.

"Yeah, yeah, I was running late. Get in here," she replied as she pulled me inside and closed the door behind me.

I followed her through the kitchen and into the living room where a notebook and pen sat on the footstool. Flopping down on the couch, I grabbed the supplies and got ready to take notes. She took the chair to my right and turned it around to face me.

"Okay, so tell me again what I'm doing here?" I asked.

She sighed. "I told you. I want to plan a dinner for the wedding party to make everybody bond."

I tapped the pen against my chin. "Riiiiiight…"

"You hardly know Daniella or Mandy, and you don't like my cousins Alyssa and Katherine." She wagged a finger at me.

"The ones who referred to the reception after your mom's funeral as 'the after party'?"

Her lips twitched. "That was Bruno, actually. But yes, they agreed with his assessment."

"Where are you thinking of having this soiree?" I asked, ignoring her comments about her cousins.

"Well, at first, I was thinking of having it at a restaurant but the more I think about it, the more it makes sense to have it here. That way everyone can really mingle and get to know each other better."

"True, that makes sense," I said diplomatically. In fact, it was the last thing I wanted to plan or attend, but Mela was my best friend and her day should be perfect. If that meant I had to be nice to a few stuck-up cousins, I would manage it.

She eyed me. "We haven't had much of a chance to talk since the party."

"That's true, I've been busy with work," I said.

"How was seeing Lucas after all this time?" She got right to the point. It was something I both loved and hated about her.

I flinched when she said his name. "It was…fine."

"Fine? I mean *he* was fine. Muscles upon muscles now." She waved her hands in the air like she was drawing his silhouette.

"Mel," I warned.

"What? I'm just saying. He was cute before but now he's… something else." She waggled her eyebrows.

"You can't be serious. You're team Lucas now?"

She scoffed. Knowing that I needed some mood stabilizer to endure the questions she would ask, I stood abruptly and went to the kitchen to fix myself a drink, pouring a heavy dose of vodka into some Clamato juice.

"Really, Liv? Day drinking? It's 11 a.m." Her lips were pursed when I returned.

"It's noon somewhere." I shrugged and took a big swig, sitting back down.

She shook her head. "For the record, I'm team Liv. I will always be team Liv. And I'm still mad as hell at Lucas *and* Nate. But I also saw the look on his face when he stared at you, and how pitiful he was after you left."

I didn't answer. There was nothing I could say to that.

"What should I serve?" She looked at the notebook in my hand pointedly.

"Food wise?" I questioned, grateful for the subject change. She nodded. "Probably best to have easy to grab foods if you want us to be able to sit around and chat. Maybe some finger foods?"

"Yeah, maybe. We could always just get a bunch of pizzas. It doesn't have to be fancy." She didn't miss my eyebrow raise. "Not everyone is as stuck up as my cousins," she said defensively.

"So, you admit they're stuck up…"

She gave me a look that shut me right up. I took another sip of my cocktail.

"What's going on with you?" Her voice was full of concern.

"What? Because I think your cousins are stuck up?"

Mela waved me off. "Everyone knows they are. That's not what I'm talking about. Talk to me about Lucas or G.G. or, hell, even your sister blowing back into town to make you a Jesus freak. You're like a clam these days."

Her eyes were piercing through me, and I shifted in my seat.

"I'm fine. Everything is fine." I shrugged like it was no big deal.

"We've been friends too long for you to sit there and lie to my face, Liv," she snapped. "You're very clearly not fine, and I wish you'd stop acting like you don't give a crap about anything or anyone. You're being so hard on everyone and pushing people away when you're the one who clearly needs help."

"I'm f—"

Mela cut me off. "If you say fine, I'm going to lose it," she warned.

I threw my hands up. "Fine. I'm not fine, okay? Does that make you happy?"

This time, she eyed me for a long while before whispering, "Of course not."

My eyes filled with tears, and I was getting really tired of crying all the time. Finally, I lost my steam and my shoulders slumped as I let a single tear slide down my cheek. "You're right. I am trying to act easy breezy like nothing fazes me but the truth is…deep down, I'm broken. It feels like my heart was ripped right out of my chest and torn to pieces and I'm just trying to glue it back together. I'm hurting, and I know I'm hurting others, but I can't seem to help myself." The confession made me think I deserved another sip.

Mela side-eyed the drink in my hand and again pressed her lips together, which meant that she wanted to say something about it but chose not to. "You've been through a lot these last few weeks. Losing G.G. was hard. It must have felt like losing one of the few connections to yourself that you have," she said quietly.

She was right. That was exactly how it felt.

"And then Lucas coming back into the picture must have felt like a huge shock. Has he told you anything?"

"No. He wouldn't say a thing about where he's been or why he left or why he never even responded to my letter."

She moved to sit beside me on the couch. The scent of her

perfume accompanied her and, with it, a sense of calm. She grabbed my hand.

"I'm so sorry, Liv. That must be painful." It wouldn't be like Mela to leave it at that, though. She had navigated the illness and loss of her own mother when she was way too young for such grief, and she wasn't about to let me get away with a pity party. Her tone shifted to a harder one. "You can't keep doing this, though. You need to start cleaning up your messes before they leave a trail of destruction you can't come back from. I get that you're hurting, I do. But it's the choices we make in the midst of our pain that really define who we are. Don't let this change you into someone I know you're not."

She gave me a little shake, as if I were a bottle of medicine that needed to mix better, got up and went down the hall to get dressed, leaving me alone with my thoughts.

14

LUCAS

I was having a very lazy Saturday. It was Halloween but that didn't mean much to me, aside from having a bowl of candy beside my door in case any kids decided to knock. I didn't want to be *that* apartment.

Nate's parents had sent over a bed, dresser, television, entertainment unit for said television, a comfy chair I had never seen before, a footstool for the couch, and a kitchen table complete with chairs, which was odd considering I hadn't had a table in my room at their place. They'd single handedly furnished my entire apartment and refused to let me pay for any of it.

I'd grumbled at Nate when he'd dropped by with his allegedly old Playstation 5; it looked so new I was pretty sure he'd just taken it out of the box before heading upstairs. It was their way of showing love, but it was a little overwhelming at times.

Thoughts of Liv continued to pepper my mind every few minutes despite trying to keep it busy with incessant shoot-em-up movies. Somehow even *Die Hard* was making me think of her. Apparently, my decision to let her go was not one my subconscious agreed with. Maybe I'd go for a run or something. That usually helped to clear my head.

A knock at the door interrupted my thoughts and had me glancing at my watch since it was only the middle of the afternoon. I opened the door and Casey was standing there—and it was the last thing I had expected. The thought of her hadn't even entered my mind in at least two years.

She was a girl I'd spent some time with before going to prison—a friend of Dylan's, but we hadn't talked since I'd left. For a second I thought she must have been there by mistake.

"Lucas, hi," she said with a smile. "I'm sorry to just show up like this. Your brother told me where you lived, and I wanted to talk to you."

I nodded and cleared my throat. "Casey, hi. Uh, how are you?"

"I'm good. Could we come in?" she asked.

It was then that I noticed the child standing behind her. "Oh, sure. Yeah, of course." I shook my head to clear it and moved out of the way.

She stepped into the apartment tentatively, shooting me an apologetic glance. The child who had the same blond hair she had and blue eyes with a touch of hazel, toddled in behind her. I guessed he was hers, and this surprised me, though she was the same age as my brother. Maybe she had settled down.

Casey cleared her throat a few times. "Could I get a glass of water?"

"Yeah, sure." I was trying not to sound as awkward as I felt.

Hurrying to the kitchen, I grabbed a clean glass from the cupboard and filled it with water from the fridge as I racked my brain for why she'd be here after all this time. Did it have to do with Dylan? Sure, we'd dated briefly—but she'd always been his friend, not mine. I handed her the glass and gestured for her to sit on the couch while I took the chair. Her son was holding on to her leg and clutching a little toy car in his chubby fingers.

Casey took a sip of water like she was somehow drawing the courage to speak from it. Her nervousness was making me uneasy.

"Does he want anything to drink?" I gestured to her son.

"I brought him some juice," she said softly and dug around in her bag until she found it. Then she handed it to him and said, "You're probably wondering why I'm here."

The thought had crossed my mind. "Is it something to do with Dylan?" I asked, as it was all I could think of.

She shook her head and took another sip of water, her hand trembling a little. "There's really no easy way to say this, Lucas. I have a son, as you can see," she started.

My eyebrows creased together with confusion. What did this have to do with me?

"His name is Luke. I named him after his father." After a pause, she added, "After you. You're the father, Lucas." She breathed out the last words like their weight had been pinning her down.

I stared at her without blinking. What had she just said? A coldness I'd never experienced began snaking its way through my guts. My eyes fell on the little boy looking at me curiously with his wide blue and hazel eyes. I looked back at her and her mouth was moving as though she was speaking, but I couldn't hear anything except the ringing in my ears.

"That can't be true," I muttered, more to myself than to her.

"It is true," she replied. The sound of her voice was muffled in my ears as if I was underwater and she was speaking above me. That seemed accurate since it felt like I was drowning.

"Just give me a second," I whispered as I stood up and sped to the bathroom.

The ice in my gut had turned to molten lava as I gripped the sink and stared at my reflection. My eyes were so wide it was almost comical, but there was nothing funny about this situation. I watched a bead of sweat trickle down the side of my face, and I turned on the cold water to splash my cheeks and forehead. Letting the water continue to run, I watched it swirl around the drain and forced myself to take deep breaths to slow down my heart rate.

How could I have a son I knew nothing about? As if on cue, I heard his laughter carry from the living room. I had lost all concept of time and had no idea how long I'd been holed up in there. Eventually, a gentle tap at the door brought me back to the present.

"Lucas? Are you going to come out sometime soon?" Casey asked from the other side of the door.

"Mommy, why we here?" Luke asked her quietly.

"I'll be right out," I called, my voice hoarse. Splashing a bit more water on my face, I turned off the tap and the silence that followed was deafening.

True: Why was she here? To tell me, and…what, exactly?

This was going to ruin my life; I wasn't ready to be a dad. Shooting a glance at myself in the mirror, my reflection seemed to taunt me and say, "Well, you are one, so get it together."

Liv's face flashed through my mind—this was going to destroy any hope I'd had of us ever getting back together. I couldn't hide in my bathroom all day, so I left and walked back into the living room where Casey sat on the couch and Luke played with several toy cars at her feet. She looked up at me with a hopeful expression on her face.

I slowly walked over to where they were and kneeled on the floor close to the little boy. He eyed me curiously as I took him in as though for the first time. His eyes had a touch of hazel in them—like mine—and the signature O'Connell yellow ring around the center of his irises. That alone wasn't enough to convince me that I was his father, but there were other signs. I knew if I pulled out a baby picture of me and my brothers, Luke would look like one of us. His face was the same shape, and he even had the weird fold at the top of his ear like we did. He was my flesh and blood, there was no denying it.

I stood up and walked to the other side of the room for some distance. "Why would you not tell me this? You know my brother, he could have gotten word to me," I whispered in frustration. "He's what? Two years old? And has no father?"

Her eyes flashed at the reprimand. "What did you want me to do? You got arrested! Was I supposed to take him to see you in...prison?" She mouthed the last word and then went on. "Is that really how you would have wanted your son to meet you?" She sighed. "You don't know how lonely the last two years have been, Lucas. When I found out I was pregnant I..." She trailed off and took a few moments to gather herself before speaking again. "I-I can't explain it, really. I just...I knew I could never have an...abortion." She exhaled sharply as though the mere word brought her physical pain. "You know my dad has money so that...that isn't the problem. It's not what I'm here for."

I could not formulate a question that made sense, so I just waited.

There was a heaviness in her gaze. "I don't need money from you, but you're right, he does need a dad. You're a good man, Lucas, you always have been. You just did something wrong, and now you've paid for it. Should our son have to grow up without a dad because of that?" Her eyes filled with tears, and I looked down at Luke whose head was darting back and forth from her to me.

She motioned to Luke with her eyes. "We need to talk to him, he's getting scared." Her hand touched his shoulder gently as she spoke softly to him. "Luke, honey, aren't you gonna drink your juice?" He nodded eagerly as though he'd forgotten he'd been holding it all the time, and Casey popped the straw in for him. He gripped it with one hand and continued holding his car with the other while he sucked back the entire contents of the juice box without taking his eyes off mine.

It felt forced to smile, but I didn't want him to be afraid of me. He spilled a little juice on his Paw Patrol t-shirt and some on the floor, and he looked down at the mess and back at me. I gave him an encouraging smile and shrugged my shoulders. Walking over to where he sat, I wiped my foot over the spill letting my sock absorb the juice.

"All gone," I said softly.

He looked at the floor as though to see for himself that it was really gone, and a slow smile spread across his face. His cheeks were rosy from the exertion of guzzling his juice box so quickly.

"Show Lucas your car, honey. He's so proud of the new car he just got." The last part was directed to me. Luke held up his car to show me and I sat down on the floor beside him to admire it.

It was a lot to take in, but what had happened wasn't Casey's fault. Not really. And it definitely wasn't *Luke's* fault. I thought we'd been careful. She had been on birth control, but since a little boy was sitting in front of me, it clearly hadn't worked. She'd raised him this whole time, with no help from me while I'd been in prison. I gave her a tight smile and a flash of relief crossed her face.

"I really am sorry, Lucas. He should know his dad, it's not fair on a boy not to have a dad."

I don't know if the pang I felt then was of shock or regret.

"Can I play with one of your cars?" I asked him gently.

He considered me for a moment and picked one up, dropping it into my hand. I pretended to drive it straight into the couch and made exaggerated crashing sounds. He looked up at me and giggled, so I did it again and he laughed even harder. Warmth began to build in my chest as I took in my son sitting before me. My. Son. That was going to take some getting used to.

"Mo," he said as he looked at me with an expectant gaze.

I glanced at Casey questioningly and she whispered, "More. He wants you to do it again."

I crashed the car into the side of the couch again and his laughter filled the apartment. The sound brought a genuine smile to my face. We played like that for another hour and eventually they left, but we had made a plan to see each other again soon.

Later, I flopped down on the couch and tried to make sense of what had just happened. Images of Casey, whom I actually hardly knew, Luke, and then Liv were swirling around in my mind like a kaleidoscope, so fast I started to feel sick.

My foot hit something hard, bringing me back to the present, and bending down, I found one of Luke's cars just under the couch. As I stared at it, I remembered being little and playing with the few toys I had—without a dad to play with me. Luke was an innocent bystander in all this, and though it was not how I would have imagined becoming a father, it wasn't something I could now change—or would run away from.

She was right. I'd grown up without a dad, and it was awful. I didn't want that for him. I had a son; he was gentle, generous with his toys, and had a laugh that lit up the whole room. I had a son, and I wasn't going to bail on him.

15

OLIVIA

You need to start cleaning up your messes before they leave a trail of destruction you can't come back from.

Mela's words replayed in my head. Maybe I *had* been too quick to throw people away. Lucas, my sister, even Ali, to an extent. A wave of guilt crashed over me. I didn't *want* to leave a trail of destruction everywhere I went, but I was acting like a wounded animal that bit anyone who approached it—even if they were there to help.

Had Lucas told me why he left? No. But had I really given him the time and space to do so? Also no. *Damn it.* Mela was probably right—she usually was. Maybe I'd consider putting a stop to my trail of destruction, but first, coffee. I was too hungover to make emotional decisions. After a quick shower, I threw my hair up into a messy bun, put on my comfiest sweatpants and a cleanish t-shirt, and headed to Brew.

It wasn't a far walk, so I opted for the fresh air instead of taking my car. I drank so much lately that my car didn't see a lot of weekend action, as I refused to drive if I'd had even a sip of alcohol. I also wasn't clear on how much alcohol remained in one's system from the night before. To play it safe, when hungover I usually stayed home or walked.

My phone buzzed in my pocket, and when I saw the text from my sister I sighed.

Praying for you. Love you.

I was about to ignore it when I remembered that I was trying *not* to leave a trail of destruction everywhere so instead I wrote back.

Thanks.

It wasn't exactly inviting, but I didn't *want* to invite more texts of that nature. I felt it was a decent compromise as I walked into Brew. A few minutes later, I sat down in a booth sipping my blended coffee drink with extra whipped cream. It was more dessert than coffee, but it did the trick.

For a mid-morning on Sunday, the cafe was not too busy. The rush from the after-church folk would start in an hour or two, and I planned to be long gone by then.

I was debating ordering some food, unsure if my stomach could handle something solid, when I looked up and watched Lucas walk through the door. My heart skipped a few beats before returning to a relatively normal rhythm as he moved to the counter and ordered something. He was wearing jeans and a light blue t-shirt, and his expression seemed guarded. I still couldn't believe how much stronger he'd grown since he'd left.

I noticed a jerkiness to his movements that made me think he was stressed about something. A new wave of guilt came over me, and I fleetingly wondered if I had anything to do with it—then chided myself for being so arrogant as to think I had any effect on him. Still, I knew I should at least apologize.

As he moved to leave, I called his name. He turned and looked for whoever was calling him. His eyes widened in surprise as he saw me and he pointed to himself questioningly as though I couldn't possibly mean him. I smirked despite myself and nodded, so he made his way over to me.

"Do you want to sit down?" I asked, second-guessing myself.

His mouth turned up in my favorite crooked smile, and I nearly dropped my drink all over my lap. He pretended not to notice but I saw something like amusement behind his eyes as he took a seat across from me.

"This is a surprise," he said, still smiling.

"I bet it is," I said with a laugh.

He drank some of his iced coffee and we sat in silence for a few moments before I broke it.

"I uh, wanted to apologize for how I acted at the engagement party."

"Liv, you have nothing to apologize for," he said quickly.

Toying with the paper wrapper from my straw, I started ripping pieces off absentmindedly.

"I didn't have to be so mean. The words I spoke were meant to hurt you, and for that I'm sorry."

A pile of ripped paper was growing on the table, and I stared down at my hands. He placed his hand on mine and I flinched but didn't pull it away.

"Liv," he said so quietly that I looked up. "It's forgiven. Friends?" He extended his hand to shake mine and I laughed.

"Friends," I replied as I shook his hand.

I could feel his gaze on me and when I looked up, it was as if I was seeing him for the first time. I knew that I'd probably never not be attracted to him, but I was seeing something deeper. A man who must have had his reasons for the things he did and the way he disappeared. The fact was, I knew him well enough to know he wasn't intentionally cruel and he probably didn't hurt me on purpose. I'd simply been a casualty on his path of destruction.

"Can I ask you something?" he said.

"Okay."

"What happened to running? I thought your dream was the Olympics someday."

I didn't want to talk about it. Having to tell him in particular about the accident felt like torture.

"Nate didn't tell you?"

"You know Nate. He doesn't like to tell—"

"Other people's stories. I should've guessed."

"You don't have to tell me if you don't want to. It's okay." He leaned back in his seat with such an apologetic look on his face that I felt badly for not just telling him.

"It was an accident during a race. I was running the hundred-meter hurdles and was out in front. On the very last hurdle, in some random fluke, my leg got caught up in it and the way I fell shattered my ankle. After my surgery, they told me I'd never run competitively again."

"Crap, Liv. I'm so sorry." His eyes were wide with shock.

I swallowed the lump in my throat. "Yeah, it sucked. A lot. It *was* my dream to compete in the Olympics, and I was starting to get noticed by some brands. Even did a few commercials. But I lost all of that when I lost the ability to run. And then when G.G. died…"

He cut in. "G.G. *died*? When?"

"Three weeks before the engagement party."

His eyes registered understanding.

"And then I ambushed you. I am so sorry; I had no idea. I wouldn't have gone," he said.

"It's fine, Lucas. At least seeing you didn't make me go on a drunken rampage like I did at G.G.'s funeral."

"You did?" He winced.

"I did. It wasn't my finest moment."

"Why, though? It's not exactly your character to do something like that."

He had no idea…

"I've changed a lot," I said.

"Yeah. No, you're right. I guess I don't really know you anymore," he said.

"It wasn't for nothing, though." I told him about Ali and Sheila's ambush.

He leaned back in his seat and looked up at the ceiling like he was attempting to stop himself from saying something he might regret. "So, they haven't changed, I guess," he finally said.

"Not in the least. That wasn't even the worst part, to be honest. The funeral was so…stuffy. People talked about G.G. like they didn't even know her. They didn't talk about her humor, or her sass. Or the way she could hold on to a grudge like no one I've ever known. They didn't talk about her generous heart or how bad she was at Euchre." I was fighting to keep it together.

"Or about her love of shrimp sauce?"

Lucas's eyes crinkled as he said it, and I burst into tears.

I put my head between my arms on the table and sobbed as quietly as I could, willing myself to stop but being unable to control the flood of emotion. And then Lucas was sliding into my side of the booth and wrapping his arms around me. I turned almost instinctively into his shoulder and wrapped my arms around his waist as he held me tightly and let me weep.

"I'm sorry," I wailed between sobs, not sure if I was apologizing for crying, for the way I'd treated him at the party, or for getting hammered at G.G.'s funeral. It was possible that I was apologizing for it all.

"Shhhh," he said soothingly as he kept one arm around me and rubbed my back with the other. "Just let it out, Liv. I'm here. I'm not going anywhere."

When I finally got a hold of myself, I was mortified. I tried to pull out of his arms, but his grip tightened.

"Don't, Liv. Don't pull away because you're embarrassed. You probably wouldn't even be this vulnerable if it wasn't for me in the first place. I am so sorry for my role in your unhappiness." It was as if he'd been holding in these words for a long time.

"Lucas—" My voice sounded terrible. I tried again. "You hurt me when you left, but I hurt you way before that. I think maybe we should just move on. Move *forward*," I clarified, speaking into his chest since he hadn't released me.

"Can I tell you something?" he asked.

"Yes."

"My feelings for you have never changed, Liv. Not after we broke up, not after you moved to New York, and not over the last couple of years without seeing you. I've never felt this way about anyone, and I know that I don't deserve a second chance, but I'm selfish enough to hope for one anyway. There is nothing in the world I want more than to make things up to you, and I hope that someday I'll be able to."

His confession done, he loosened his grip on me, giving me a chance to escape if I wanted to.

I didn't move. As I stayed glued to his chest, I felt his shoulders relax. I breathed in his familiar scent of sunshine mixed with body wash and shampoo. My face would be blotchy and disgusting, so I kept it buried while he ran his fingers up and down my arm. It was the most peaceful I'd been in weeks, and though I was trying very hard not to feel anything, a seed of hope broke open within me and I felt it take root.

16

LUCAS

"Why didn't you tell Liv?" Nate was staring at me while holding a screwdriver in midair. It was Friday after work and he'd come over to help me baby proof the apartment.

"I don't know, man; I panicked. She was crying and I just...I panicked."

"Why was she crying?" He squinted at me.

"I didn't *make* her cry, if that's what you're asking." I threw him a look and stood up to admire my handiwork as he finished installing the last child-safety lock on the cupboard under the sink.

Luke was coming over for his first overnight visit and I was nervous. I'd probably gone completely overboard with the safety measures. There was a doorknob cover on every door, a latch on every drawer, and a lock on every cabinet. I'd even put corner cushions on my kitchen table, all-purpose safety straps on my fridge so it couldn't be opened, and I'd tied down anything that could fall like my dresser.

"You planning on bubble-wrapping the kid too?" Nate asked with a smirk.

"Hilarious. The kid's name is Luke." I looked at my watch.

"Aren't you supposed to be meeting Mela to beg for her forgiveness or something?"

"Looks like you're the comedian today." He handed the screwdriver back to me. "Seriously, though—you'd better tell Liv about this sooner than later because if she finds out from someone else, it's going to blow up in your face." He shook his head before taking off.

I should have told Liv about Luke, but she had been so vulnerable, I hadn't found the moment. Yet I realized how unfair it was of me to profess my feelings for her and my desire for another chance without disclosing the fact that I had a son. Not only did I have a son, but I was going to be in his life, caring for him, spending time with him, being there for him. I was a dad now.

In my defense, I had known for less than twenty-four hours at the time, but I still felt like a piece of crap about it. Nate was right. I needed to tell her, and I would. Just as soon as I figured out how to.

A knock at the door brought me out of my thoughts, and I opened it to find Casey with Luke and a couple overnight bags in her arms. It seemed like I wasn't the only one preparing too much.

"Hey, Lucas." Casey beamed up at me and I smiled back politely.

"Hey." I moved aside to let them in.

Casey glanced around with an approving look on her face. "I'm impressed. You really covered all your safety bases here." She stepped into the living room holding Luke in her arms. "Where should we set up?"

"We?" A sinking feeling washed over me.

"Yeah, we. I'm spending the night too," she said it as if she was letting me know the weather forecast. *It's going to rain tomorrow; by the way, I'm sleeping over.*

"No, you're not," I said defensively. It was weird that she was planning to spend the night at my place. We hadn't discussed anything like that, and she'd gone ahead and packed an overnight bag for herself?

She looked slightly confused. "I hope you can understand, Lucas. He's too little to sleep here without me. We've never spent a night apart before. My hope is that he can get used to you little by little, and then you two can be alone."

I blew out my breath. When she put it like that it was understandable, but I still wasn't thrilled at the idea. I plopped down on the chair. "You two can sleep in my room, and I'll take the couch."

She nodded, though I thought I saw something like disappointment cross her face.

"I just..." I started then paused, wondering if what I was about to say was necessary. "There's someone else, and I care for her very much."

Her brows creased in confusion. "Okay..." she said as though my words were nonsensical.

Perhaps I was an idiot who had entirely misread the situation. "Sorry, just ignore me," I said with a forced laugh. She smiled in response and didn't bring it up again.

Any doubts I might have had were relieved as we spent the rest of the day together without incident. We explored a park by my apartment, much to Luke's delight, and I made dinner for them, strapping Luke to a booster seat and cutting up his food into the smallest pieces I could. Casey let me put him to bed in the little pack & play she had brought with her, and I read him some books she'd packed until he fell asleep. I tiptoed out so as not to wake him. All in all, it had been a good day.

I came back out to where Casey was sitting on the couch playing on her phone and joined her, unsure of what we were supposed to do now that Luke was asleep.

"You were great with him tonight," she said.

"I was, wasn't I?" I replied, making her laugh.

"You really were. I'm impressed." She inched closer to me on the couch.

I stood up and moved to the chair, not caring if my move was obvious. She was a short, slight woman, but her presence had me on guard for reasons I couldn't explain.

"Do you want to watch a movie?" she asked.

"I'm actually pretty tired." I hoped she'd get the hint and go to my room.

"It's like eight p.m.," she said with a laugh.

Checking my watch, I saw that she was right and grimaced. "Oh."

"It's just a movie, Lucas." She put her hands up innocently.

"I'll make some popcorn," I said, going to the kitchen.

I was tense the entire movie, sitting defensively on the chair. I wasn't even sure what we'd watched when the credits started rolling.

Finally, she stood to move to the bedroom, yawned and stretched. Her shirt rode up, making me look away so fast I nearly injured my neck.

"Night, Lucas," she said with a small smile, and closed the door to my bedroom behind her.

Grabbing a blanket and spare pillow from the linen closet, I set up the couch, sent Liv a goodnight text, plugged my phone in, and lay fully clothed in sweatpants and a t-shirt. It took me a long time to fall asleep—and when I did, I was ambushed by dreams of Liv.

Her soft silky hair in my hands, the way she sighed when I kissed her, the feel of her pressed against my chest as I pulled her body close to mine… I awoke with a gasp as someone's lips pressed against mine.

They sure as hell weren't Liv's.

"What the hell, Casey?" I pushed her off me and she toppled off the couch.

Flipping on the light, I glared at her as her cheeks flushed. She was in short shorts and a tank top that left nothing to the imagination.

I looked away as I said angrily, "Why would you do that, knowing that there was someone else?"

"I'm so sorry, Lucas." She kneeled back on the couch, looking the picture of innocence but still half naked. "Seeing you with Luke all day has made me realize how much I want us to be a family more than anything. I've been so lonely, and…and I miss you."

"Casey, it's not like that between us," I said firmly. "We haven't seen each other in years, and before that, not even for long. You know it."

"But it could be good, Lucas. Can't you see that? We were happy once. We could be again," she said hopefully.

Happy? Either she remembered things very differently or she had convinced herself of some fantasy scenario. But I couldn't remind her we had been *casual*. She was the mother of my child now.

"Look, I'm really sorry that you had Luke alone. If I'd known, I would have done everything I could to be there for you both. I'll still be there for Luke—that won't ever change. But I'm in love with someone else, Casey, and I can't live a lie."

Her eyes were downcast as she spoke. "You loved her before me, then?" She sounded close to tears.

And she gave me no choice but to be clear. "I never…loved you, Casey. I never meant for you to think that. I thought we both wanted the same thing—companionship." A tightness grew in my stomach; none of this was easy, and I didn't mean to cause pain, but to leave things unclear would only create more problems.

She stayed quiet for a long time, staring down at her folded hands in her lap. Eventually, she spoke again, and I had to strain to hear her. "Are you with her now then?"

Warning bells were going off in my brain. How was I supposed to tell her I wasn't even with Liv when she was asking for us to be a family? "Not…exactly," I said carefully.

Her head snapped up. "You're not together? Why? If you

love this woman, why aren't you with her?" She studied my face with no trace of malice.

"It's complicated. I messed up by not being completely honest with her about some things, and now I'm trying to make it right. But just because we're not together, doesn't mean my heart isn't hers."

A single tear slid down her cheek. "What is she like?"

The question caught me off guard.

"Liv? She's…" I trailed off realizing that no good could come of this conversation. "I don't want to hurt you, Casey."

"Too late for that, Lucas," she replied. There was no bitterness in her tone, just a quiet resignation. "Does she know about Luke?"

A pang of guilt made me fumble for words for a second. "Not yet, but I'm planning to tell her soon."

"Do you think she'll accept that you have a child? It's important for me to know."

The Liv I knew was kind and compassionate; I had to believe that she'd try. "I think she will. Listen, it's late. I'm going to try to get some more sleep before Luke wakes up."

Without another word, she got up off the couch and made her way back to my room, silently closing the door behind her.

I tossed and turned the rest of the night, continuously waking up with a start as if someone might be standing over me. One thing I knew for sure: Casey was never spending the night at my place again.

In the morning, I woke up to Luke prying my eyelid open.

"Hey, buddy," I mumbled incoherently.

"Hi," he shouted in my face as he rolled one of his cars over my head.

I threw off the blanket and sat up. Casey came out of my bedroom fully dressed, thank goodness, and dropped down on the chair.

"Morning," she said, not making eye contact with me.

"Morning."

"Is there a Starbucks around here?" she asked.

"Yeah, but it's a good ten-minute drive."

"Would you mind going to get some egg bites for Luke? It's his favorite breakfast, and we always get it on the weekend."

"Oh. Uh, sure."

After quickly changing into jeans and a clean t-shirt, I grabbed my car keys and left the apartment. I needed a good shot of caffeine anyway.

17

OLIVIA

"Are you sure, Carrie? I don't mind coming to help set things up," I told my boss.

"It's fine, we've totally got this. Plus, you haven't had a Saturday completely off in a while. Take a nap, enjoy life. I'll live vicariously through you and see you tomorrow." She laughed at my hesitation and hung up before I could argue.

I guess I have the day off.

Sudden inspiration had me texting Lucas to see if he was free to hang out. The thought of his embrace the week before had set me on edge, and I still wasn't sure if that was a good or bad thing. Maybe I was foolish to entertain the idea of giving him a second chance. There was only one way to find out.

Thanks for the goodnight text, I was already asleep. Are you free this morning? I suddenly have the day off and thought maybe we could hang out.

Seeing the dots after a while made my heart flutter. He was writing back.

Why don't you come over?

My mind went into overdrive at the thought of being alone with him in his apartment. I wasn't sure we were ready for that.

Can't we meet somewhere?

His reply came back quickly.

I'm just finishing up some chores and then we can walk to a place nearby. I think you'll like it.

THAT SEEMED REASONABLE. I texted him back to agree and ask for his address.

It turned out he lived a couple minutes away, so I drove right over since I had already been ready to head into work. I knew the building from visiting my high school friends Adam and Isabel, and baby Nori. It was still rundown, but that had never bothered me. I'd probably have moved in there myself if an apartment had been available at the time. I climbed the stairs slowly while I argued with myself.

We're friends, just friends. Why did he ask me to pick him up from his apartment though? What am I going to do if he wants to kiss me? Maybe I should stay in the hallway. Am I even ready for this?

Before I was ready, I was outside his door. I took a deep breath and knocked. It swung open, and a woman who looked a few years older than me stood in the doorway with a towel on her head like she'd just come out of the shower. She was holding a child.

She gazed at me expectantly.

"Oh, I'm sorry. I must have the wrong apartment." I laughed with embarrassment as I looked around the hallway.

"Are you looking for Lucas?" she asked with a smile.

I stared at her for a long second before answering. "Um, yeah, I am, actually."

"He's just out getting his son a little treat," she said as she nodded to the little blond-haired boy who was looking at me curiously behind hazel blue eyes.

"His *s-son?*" I stammered. This wasn't happening. *How much did I drink last night?* I asked myself before remembering that I'd stayed home and sober for once.

"Yeah, of course. I take it he didn't tell you?" She smiled sadly, as if she pitied me.

I could do nothing but shake my head.

"That is just so Lucas, isn't it? Gosh. Well, anyway, would you like to come in and wait for him? He shouldn't be too much longer," she offered pleasantly as the child squirmed in her arms, wanting to climb down.

"No!" I practically shouted then collected myself. "Sorry, no. I wouldn't want to intrude on your f-family time." I stuttered on the word family as I took a step back.

"What's your name?" she asked.

"Olivia."

She set the child down and he ran around the apartment making wee-woo sounds like he was an ambulance. Glancing at him with pure adoration, she laughed. "He's just like his dad. Did you want me to tell Lucas that you came by, Olivia? I'm Casey, by the way." Her lips curved slightly like she had a secret. She wasn't the only one, apparently.

"Oh, no. That won't be necessary. Again, I'm so sorry to have barged in on you guys like this. It won't happen again," I said the last part quietly. I'd been such a fool, but I wasn't going to fall apart in front of this stranger.

"It was nice to meet you, Olivia," she said as she closed the door.

I hurried down the hallway and took the stairs two at a time, then flew through the door to get outside. Sitting in my car, I took deep breaths to pull myself together.

His words from the party came back to me. *There are… things…that kept us apart. That kept me away from you.* "Things" weren't human beings. I never would have imagined that a child was the *thing* that had kept him away from me. A whole damn family all cozied up in his apartment. Is that why he'd asked me to go there? So I could see it all for myself?

A car pulled into the lot and I sank in my seat when I saw that it was Lucas. He looked exhausted and didn't even notice me as he jogged to the building and went inside. Probably eager to get back to his real life, I thought bitterly. I was such an idiot.

Hot tears of rage pooled in my eyes and slid down my cheeks as I started the car and drove away.

How could he have kept a child secret from me? A human being should never be kept a secret. Too many emotions were making their way into my chest, making it feel as though I was being ripped apart from the inside. There was only one way I knew how to turn them off, and that involved a whole hell of a lot of alcohol.

Fool me once, shame on you—but fool me this many times? Shame on me.

18

LUCAS

I pulled out my phone and sent Liv yet another text, attempting to get a response out of her. The last time she had messaged me was two weeks ago.

> Lucas, we can't be friends. I've been thinking about things a lot, and I need a clean break. I'm tired of having a broken life with nothing but dead ends before me. Please let me go.

I had sent her a dozen messages begging her to reply to me, but I'd heard nothing back. All my calls went straight to voicemail. I couldn't figure out what had changed. We'd had such a powerful moment at Brew, and I thought she might consider giving me a second chance. The text from her before then had been playful, thanking me for comforting her. And then she froze me out without warning.

Today was one of my visit days with Luke, and we had just gotten back from the park near my place. Since his first overnight visit two weeks ago, I'd seen him a few times, just the two of us.

I stood in the kitchen trying to decide between mac & cheese or chicken fingers for lunch when a knock at the door surprised me. As hopeful as I was that it might be Liv, I also didn't want it to be her right this second considering Luke was there. I hurried over to the door and swung it open. To my surprise, my brother stood awkwardly in the hallway.

"Hey, Dyl," I said in confusion. "Didn't I tell you I had Luke today?" I had informed him of Luke's existence over Thanksgiving.

He ran his hand over the stubble on his chin. "Yeah, you mentioned it. I thought I'd come by and finally meet the little squirt. He is my family too, right?" He stepped past me into the apartment.

Luke stood looking at us.

"Hey, Luke, this is your Uncle Dylan. Can you say Uncle Dylan?"

"Unc Diwin." He said like it was a mouthful. And it sort of was.

"Good job, dude," I said encouragingly.

He dumped his bucket of cars on the floor in front of my couch and I plopped on the ground to play our favorite game. I drove one of the cars into the couch with a dramatic crash, making Luke laugh loudly with a silly face.

Dylan watched us with a pensive look on his face before joining us on the floor. He grabbed one of the cars and tentatively tried to mirror what I had done, but his crash just didn't have the flare mine did. Luke scooted into my lap as if unsure what to make of Dylan.

I laughed and then my chest tightened when his little fists bunched into my shirt and held on to me.

"Paw 'trol?" he asked looking up at me with hopeful eyes.

"You wanna watch Paw Patrol, buddy?"

He nodded eagerly, so I put it on for him and got up to make lunch. Dylan followed me into the kitchen as Luke stayed on the couch, captivated by his show.

"You've changed, you know," Dylan said.

I glanced at him as I turned on the oven and pulled the chicken fingers out of the freezer.

"Have I?"

"Yeah. You're different. More grown up."

"How do you figure?" I spread out the chicken fingers on a pan and set them aside as I waited for the oven to get to temperature.

"You just accepted responsibility for Luke with no hesitation. It's like you were born for this life. For being a dad." His tone had a thoughtful tinge to it that made me think he didn't believe he was capable of the same.

"You'd do it too, Dyl," I said, chopping up cucumber pieces. He scoffed in response. "I'm serious. Jail may have hardened me—I mean, it had to—but it also showed me what was most important."

"And what's that?"

I shrugged. "Family, friends, the people who care about you even when you screw up so badly it would be reasonable for them to abandon you. I couldn't turn my back on him. You of all people should understand that." I threw him a look as I put the chicken fingers into the oven and set a timer.

"Yeah." He ran his hands through his hair the same way I did and gave Luke another glance filled with sadness.

As Dylan made his way into the living room to sit on the couch with Luke, my thoughts drifted to Liv. Glancing into the living room, I saw my brother trying to ask Luke about his show, but the boy was too engrossed in Paw Patrol to respond. I chuckled to myself as I cut the chicken fingers into bite-sized pieces and popped Luke's plastic plate into the freezer for a minute to cool them down slightly.

Looking into the living room again, I nearly laughed out loud as my brother jingled his keys in front of Luke's face to try to get his attention. Clearly, he didn't realize that only babies liked to play with jingling keys. Luke moved farther away from him on the couch.

Dylan stood up and caught my eye. "I'm gonna take off." He still sounded off, but I just didn't have the energy to ask him about it.

"Okay, man. See you later." I pulled the plate out of the freezer and popped a piece into my mouth to check the temperature. Dylan let himself out and I locked the door behind him.

"You hungry, buddy?" I called to Luke.

"Ya," he said at a decibel that made my ears ring. He ran into the kitchen and put his arms up for me to lift him into his booster seat. I squeezed some ketchup on his plate and he began dipping his pieces into it, sucking the ketchup off, and dipping them in again.

"You've gotta eat them too, bud," I said with a laugh.

He did the same with his pieces of cucumber and ranch dip, and then he chewed dramatically with his mouth wide open and a mischievous look in his eyes. I snorted. Spending time with a two-year-old was much more enjoyable than I had anticipated. It's not how I would have chosen to enter fatherhood, but since it was here, I figured I should make the most of it.

I found myself wishing that Liv could be a part of it too, though I wasn't sure that would ever happen. No matter how hard I tried, my heart seemed unwilling and unable to give up on her. And I wasn't sure how I felt about that.

19

OLIVIA

I stepped into the shower and felt the heat begin to dissolve the tension in my shoulders. Bracing myself against the wall, I let the water pour over my head and down my back as I mentally went through my checklist for the day. *Go to work, help plan a Bar Mitzvah, get drinks with Jenny after work.* I considered wearing my evening outfit to work but thought better of it. I'd just have to bring a bigger purse to carry it and my shoes.

I took my time washing my hair and body since I'd been woken up early by a nightmare and couldn't get back to sleep. There was plenty of time before I had to be at the office. I shuddered as I recalled the way Lucas had been holding the woman from his apartment in the dream. Casey. I'd never be able to forget that name or the way she looked with her striking blue eyes, slim figure, and perfectly manicured nails. Apparently, my brain had committed her to memory, as my dream perfectly recalled every agonizing detail of her appearance. I had woken up drenched with sweat and a deep sense of loss I couldn't seem to shake.

Stepping out of the shower, I wiped the steam from the mirror and looked at my reflection. The circles under my eyes would need a lot of concealer. My face was pale and had dry patches of skin. Maybe I had been drinking too much; I really wasn't looking so hot.

I plugged in my dryer, straightened my hair, then loaded moisturizer on my face. Finally, I applied a lot more makeup than usual. Nodding at my reflection, I saw that I still had a good hour before I had to be at work, so I decided to grab a drink on the way. When I opened the door, Nate was standing there with his fist in the air, about to knock.

"Nate!" I clutched my chest and stepped backwards. "You scared the ever-loving crap out of me."

"Sorry." He chuckled, not seeming sorry at all. "Can I come in?"

I gestured for him to come in and closed the door. He was wearing sweats and his favorite hoodie. It was filled with holes, his comfort outfit.

"What's up, Nate?" I asked as he took a seat on the couch. He wouldn't have come alone if there wasn't a good reason, and that made me nervous.

"I need to tell you something, and I don't want you to freak out," he started cautiously.

"I take it this has something to do with Lucas?" I sat down on the chair across from him and fought the smile that was building from watching him squirm.

"Yeah." He sighed. "He's going to be my best man." His gaze was a mix of defiance and a little fear, like he was daring me to argue with him but hoping I wouldn't.

"Seriously, Nate? Why?"

"Come on, Liv. He's my best friend," he pleaded as he rested an ankle over his knee.

"He *was* your best friend before he disappeared for more than three years. Doesn't that bother you?"

"Sometimes there's more to a story than what's on the surface," he said, sounding a lot like some kind of philosopher.

"Do you know where he was?" I asked.

A flash of real fear came over his face, but he smoothed out his expression. "That's not what I came here to talk about," he hedged.

"That's not a no, Nate. Does Mela know you've known where he's been this whole time?"

"Liv," he warned. "Mela made me come over and tell you myself since it was my decision to ask him and she wasn't about to tell you."

"So I'll have to walk down the aisle with him?" I asked, letting him get away with the subject change.

He nodded.

"Okay, fine," I said to be rid of a tension that had me exhausted. "It'll take what, thirty seconds? I think I can manage."

"Will you still come to the dinner next week?" he asked sheepishly.

I'd forgotten about the 'bonding' dinner I'd helped Mela plan. "Of course. I'm not about to let Mela down like that. But please don't try to put us alone together or have us talk, Nate. I'm truly asking. I can't do this right now. I know you're his friend, but you're also mine, aren't you?"

"I won't." He crossed his fingers in an x over his heart as a promise.

"Did you know about Lucas's son?"

His jaw dropped. "How did—?" He stopped himself from asking how I'd found out, probably so he wouldn't have to betray my confidence or Lucas's. "He wanted to tell you, Liv. He was trying to figure out how to." The look of concern on his face made me shift in my seat.

I suppressed a bitter laugh. "Oh, he figured it out in the end."

Nate looked at me in confusion but seemed to think better of continuing that line of conversation. Looking around the apartment, he pursed his lips.

"Are all of these bottles yours?" His tone was light and curious, but his eyes told a different story. One of a friend concerned with my drinking habits.

"Mostly," I lied. They were all mine; my roommate didn't drink. But I wasn't about to admit that to Nate when his best man was a big part of why I'd been drinking so much lately.

He opened his mouth to say something then closed it.

Thinking he'd changed his mind about scolding me over my drinking habits, I stood up to put a few of the bottles into the recycling bin.

"Liv," he started sadly. "You've been drinking a lot lately. Is everything okay?"

"Nate, come on. You sound like Mela." My laugh wasn't lighthearted. It sounded more strangled than anything.

"I'm just saying—"

I cut him off. "And *I'm* just saying that it's not really your business, okay? I'm sorry, that was rude. I'm just late for work, so I've really gotta get going." I was lying and the look on his face told me that he knew it, but he stood up anyway.

"Okay. But promise me that if you need anything, you'll reach out." His eyes searched my face as we stood in my doorway.

"Sure, Nate. I promise."

He pulled me into a quick hug. "We love you, Liv."

"We?" I said, making him smile again.

"Yeah, it's part of the whole getting married thing. Apparently, we're a united front now, and we speak on behalf of each other." He shrugged as I lightly shoved him out the door.

"I'll see you at the dinner, Nate. Go cancel your seating arrangement or whatever other Team Lucas plans you and Mela were cooking up."

He rolled his eyes dramatically. "Fine, I'll go burn the flow chart."

I wasn't entirely sure he was kidding.

20

LUCAS

"Do you need me to set the table or anything?" I asked Mela, having shown up to their place early to help them set up for the dinner.

"We're going for more of a buffet-style feel, so just pile the plates beside all the food," she said coldly as she pointed.

She'd been particularly icy to me since I'd arrived, but I wasn't about to ask why for fear she might tell me. I knew she'd get around to it eventually, and it was in my best interest to wait until she was ready—and not a moment sooner.

I did as she asked, placing serving utensils beside every dish. They'd opted for Greek food, so there were salads, potatoes, dips and sauces, and all the fixings for Gyros. It all smelled amazing, but my stomach was in knots, knowing that I'd be seeing Liv for the first time since that day at Brew.

A month had passed, and I still had no idea why she had shut me out. I walked into the kitchen and accidentally interrupted a whisper-fight between Nate and Mela.

"Oh, sorry," I said, and started to back away.

Nate gave Mela a pointed look and pushed past me, leaving the two of us alone. I turned to follow him, but her voice stopped me in my tracks.

"Lucas," she spat. I stayed frozen to the spot, my shoulders tense.

"Mela?"

"How could you?"

I turned around slowly and flinched at the look on her face. In fact, following the Greek theme, I was surprised not to have turned to stone after making eye contact with her.

"You're gonna have to be a little more specific," I said while holding my hands up in defense.

She stomped over to me and stuck a finger in my face. "You have a secret family, Lucas. And then you let it drop on Liv's head like it was no big deal."

Had Nate told her? No, he wouldn't have. "I—what?"

"Don't play dumb with me. Liv went to your apartment and found your little family all nice and cozied up at your place. Your girlfriend had just gotten out of the shower, for goodness' sake!"

She was saying words, and they were definitely in English, but nothing was making sense. "What are you talking about, Mela?" Panic was climbing up my throat, and I was sure I was going to puke.

"Liv. Found. Your. Secret. Family." She said the words one at a time, with particular emphasis on the word *secret.*

"I don't have a secret family," I cried.

"So, you *don't* have a son then?"

"I do. I do, but Liv doesn't know that…yet." I could see by the look on Mela's face that I was wrong. "How did she even get my address?" I asked in shock.

She looked at me like I had two heads. "You texted it to her, ya dip."

"No, I didn't!"

"Have you been smoking pot again? Your short-term memory seems a little shot. She texted you to see if you wanted to hang out with her since she had the day off and you wrote back telling her to come over—and sent her your address. When she got there, your little girlfriend answered the door with your son in her arms and told her you were off getting him some kind of treat." She glared at me as though daring me to argue.

"I swear, Mela. I swear that I never sent her a text with my address. I've been wracking my brain for a way to tell her about my son without having her hate me. Springing it on her like that is the last thing I would ever do."

"Show me your phone," she demanded. I pulled it out and handed it over. "You don't have an unlock code?"

"I live alone. Forgot to do it." I shrugged.

She simply shook her head as she pulled up the messages between me and Liv. I watched her face as she scrolled through and winced at the pitying look she gave me after seeing all the unanswered texts I'd sent. "You're right, I don't see anything with your address," she mused.

The feeling of mounting panic turned to dread and dropped into my gut like an elevator whose cables had snapped. "What day was it?" I knew exactly what she'd say. A Sunday morning a few weeks ago. The morning after Casey and Luke had spent the night. The morning she'd sent me off to Starbucks to get Luke some egg bites. The morning after she'd kissed me in the middle of the night and I'd forgotten my phone by the couch when I left.

"I don't know. It was a Sunday morning a few weeks ago." She handed my phone back to me confirming what I'd suspected.

Had Casey…? No, she wouldn't have done something like that. And yet… What if she was way more manipulative than I had imagined?

"What is it, Lucas? What are you thinking?" Mela demanded.

"I think I know what happened, but I need to be sure," I said cautiously.

"Regardless of what happened, you still kept a monumental secret from Liv."

"I know—"

Again, she cut me off. "No, you don't *know*, Lucas. You kept a whole damn human secret from the girl you say you love. Never mind the fact that it's the kind of life-changing secret any friend should be told—have you forgotten Liv's story? She's *been* the dirty little secret, and you know how she feels about that. How is she *ever* supposed to trust you again?"

Furious as she was, Mela spoke nothing but the truth. I had screwed up—badly. There was really nothing I could say to defend myself.

"I was rooting for you, man." Her tone was full of disappointment.

Having made her point, she strode out of the kitchen, leaving me to my thoughts. Somehow, Mela's disappointment in me was the hardest pill to swallow.

No wonder Liv hadn't responded to my texts or calls. I couldn't blame her, after everything that had happened.

Then I drew myself up with a different thought. She could decide what to feel *after* I'd made her understand that there was nothing going on between me and Casey. I'd screwed up multiple times, but I was not going to let her misunderstand me again. Liv was the only woman I'd ever loved, and if nothing else, I needed her to know that.

The time told me that guests would be arriving soon. My new goal was to make Liv listen to me. Enough was enough, and I was tired of not getting through to her. I was pretty sure *her* goal would be to avoid me at all costs, but unfortunately for her, I liked a challenge.

21

OLIVIA

I walked into Mela's dinner party more than fashionably late after debating for a full hour whether I was going at all.

In the end, I remembered what I had said to Nate about not letting Mela down, so I reluctantly threw on a black dress that hung just below my knees and some matching flats. I kept my hair straight and curled the ends then applied makeup focusing heavily on the circles under my eyes. If I had to face Lucas, at least I'd look decent doing it.

My plan was still to avoid him as much as possible, but I had a nagging suspicion that his plan would be the exact opposite, considering how often he'd texted and called over the last couple of weeks. I had considered blocking his number to make it easier on myself, but in the end I just couldn't bring myself to do it.

Nate and Mela's house had been transformed into a mini version of their engagement party and I suspected they had used the same decorations. Black and gold streamers hung from the ceiling and some leftover foil balloons swayed, having lost a portion of helium. They were still cute.

I had slipped in unnoticed and snuck into the kitchen to make myself a vodka cranberry before facing anyone. I downed a couple of shots, but my plan to go unnoticed was foiled almost immediately as Lucas walked into the kitchen. Our eyes met and the air seemed to charge with electricity.

He was wearing a black collared shirt and I couldn't help but notice how well it hugged his broad shoulders. The golden ring around his irises was mesmerizing and seemed to hold me in place as he came closer. I swallowed hard as I noticed the resolute fire in his gaze and my heartrate quickened sensing how dangerous a determined Lucas might be.

"Liv," he said with surprise as I went back to mixing my drink, eyes focused on how much vodka I was pouring into my glass.

"Lucas," I replied coldly.

"We need to talk." He took another step towards me.

Just then Mela burst into the kitchen with flushed cheeks and bright eyes, obviously a few drinks ahead of me. She wore an adorable black and gold dress fit for a princess that had tulle puffed out at the bottom. "There you are," she said to me as she shot Lucas a mysterious look.

"Here I am," I said with much more enthusiasm than I felt.

She marched over to me and linked her arm in mine, then pulled me towards the dining room. I snatched my drink from the counter just in time. We walked by Lucas without a word, and I intentionally kept my eyes averted.

"You're late," Mela told me.

"I know, I'm sorry. I'm here now though," I offered.

She looked me up and down and I noted the approval that registered on her face. "I'll allow it because you look hot, and that is exactly what he deserves."

She nodded towards the kitchen; Lucas still hadn't emerged from it. I snorted as she took me to the buffet and shoved a plate in my free hand.

"Mangia!" she said in Italian, pointing at all the food.

It was quite a spread of Greek food. I loaded up on salad, made myself a Gyro and opted for a chair rather than the couch.

I sat cross legged with my plate in my lap while I chugged half my drink before taking a bite of food.

Lucas came back into the room and his eyes narrowed slightly as he took in my defensive position on the chair. I couldn't help the way my lips twitched as I tried not to laugh. Unfortunately for me, he strode right over to where I was sitting and plopped down on the floor beside me.

He rested his forearm on the chair, crowding my space. Mela pursed her lips across the room, but to my dismay she continued a conversation with her cousin Alyssa.

"Liv, I know you don't want to talk to me, but there are things you need to know," he said, his voice turning my insides to butter. He was so hard to resist, and the truth was, I didn't want to resist him; I had to. The heat from his body so close to mine was burning away the resolve I had been clinging to.

"This isn't the time or place," I said out of the side of my mouth, and finished the rest of my drink in a few gulps.

"I realize that, but you won't return my texts or calls." He was so close that I could feel his breath on my face, and I leaned towards him involuntarily.

I watched as Mela's other cousin, Katherine, got up from the couch leaving a space between the other two bridesmaids, Daniella and Mandy, and I scrambled off the chair and into the vacant seat, surprising them.

"Ladies," I said with a mouth full of salad.

"Er, hey, Liv," Daniella said politely.

"It's nice to see you," Mandy added kindly.

I swallowed my bite and made pleasant conversation with them while Lucas watched me from the floor. We were supposed to be bonding with the rest of the wedding party, after all. After a while, he got up and started chatting with a couple of Nate's groomsmen, so I took the opportunity to sneak into the kitchen and pour myself another drink.

While there, I decided that I wasn't getting drunk fast enough, so I downed a few more shots and finished making another vodka cranberry. I turned to leave and slammed into Lucas, who clearly hadn't been as distracted as I had assumed and now blocked my path. My breathing hitched at our proximity and the fact that the counter was behind me and I couldn't back away.

His eyes bore into mine intensely as he gripped the counter on either side of me, boxing me in. His gaze travelled down my face and stopped on my lips then darted back to my eyes.

"Lucas," I said breathlessly, though I'd meant to put a warning in my tone. My stupid body seemed to betray me as my chest heaved up and down, practically touching his as I struggled to catch my breath.

"I need you to listen to me."

His voice had an edge to it and his eyes flashed with intensity, as though he could make me listen by simply holding my gaze. It seemed to be working, as I stood frozen in place. The shots I had drunk weren't doing me any favors as I breathed him in. I wasn't sure which one of us leaned forward, or maybe we both did, but suddenly there was no more space between us and his lips were inches from mine.

"Mela!" I called in a panic. It was childish and I knew it, but I was seconds away from making a very bad decision and I needed someone to interrupt.

Lucas's eyes narrowed ever so slightly as Mela ran into the kitchen looking for the fire she assumed was engulfing the room. As soon as she caught sight of us, she skidded to a stop and her jaw dropped.

"What's going on, Liv?" she asked with suspicion.

Lucas had yet to free me from the cage his arms had formed around me, but the moment I struggled, he stepped back. I supposed I could have freed myself at any time instead of yelling for Mela. My cheeks flushed with embarrassment at my behavior, and I stepped away from him.

"I think we should go dancing now that everyone's eaten. There's a pretty cool club in a renovated barn that I've been to.

We could go there?" I asked Mela, still very much aware of Lucas's gaze on me.

She squealed a little and gripped my arm. "Yes, let's do that!" she slurred.

Turning back to the counter, I downed my drink and poured another shot for me and Mela. We clinked our glasses and tossed them back. I relished the burn down my throat.

"Let's go then," I said as I linked my arm with Mela's and left Lucas standing in the kitchen staring after us.

22

LUCAS

We all piled into Ubers to get to the club, which was the last place I wanted to go.

Liv had conveniently suggested guys and girls go separately, so I was crammed into a van that smelled like old cheese with Nate and the rest of the groomsmen I hardly knew. Christian, Aiden, Kyle, and Carter, I think their names were. I was pretty sure Nate knew them all from work at his parents' newly acquired publishing company, and they talked shop all the way to the club.

I would have felt left out if I hadn't been focused on trying to get Liv to talk to me. I supposed I had to be grateful for small mercies, or however the saying went.

I had tried talking to her, but the only thing that seemed to get her attention was our physical connection, so I had used it to my advantage. What I hadn't planned on was how much it would affect me too. I probably should have seen it coming, having been celibate for more than two years, but my desire for her hit me like a freight train the closer we got.

Our van pulled up behind theirs and Liv led the charge into the club without a backwards glance. I could see she was continuing to play the avoidance game and had probably suggested we go dancing so that we wouldn't be able to talk. I smiled ruefully at how far she would go to avoid a simple conversation. A subtle warning in the back of my mind told me not to push her too far, but I ignored it.

After finally climbing out of the stinky vehicle, I stayed outside for a minute to breathe in the fresh air and collect myself. I hadn't enjoyed crowds before prison and now I downright hated them. Accidentally bumping into someone behind bars meant a likely fist fight, and even though that wasn't my life anymore, I was still on edge in a crowded situation.

I followed Kyle, who had stayed behind looking a little green himself, and caught sight of Liv at the bar ordering more drinks. She and the bartender looked too familiar with each other. Liv threw her head back in laughter at something he said, and I felt a pang of jealousy in my gut. Now double fisting some drinks, she led the rest of the girls in some kind of conga line on to the dance floor.

Nate materialized beside me with drooping shoulders and an irritated expression on his face.

"This is your fault, you know," he shouted above the music gesturing to the club we were in.

I grimaced. "Yeah, I know. I'll make it up to you," I shouted back.

He rolled his eyes at me and went after Mela on the dance floor. I laughed at how awkward his moves were. Nate hated dancing, but Mela loved it; he'd never told her, knowing that she wouldn't make him go with her. *I'd rather be somewhere I hate with her than be somewhere I love without her,* he'd said once. He made a face at me, and I laughed again.

My eyes moved to Liv. She was dancing with the two bridesmaids who weren't Mela's cousins. I couldn't remember their names. Clearly the bonding dinner had been a massive success, I thought sarcastically. I considered going to grab a beer until I saw the way the bartender was watching Liv—like he was about to jump over the bar to get to her.

Feeling more possessive than I had any right to, I made my way onto the dance floor, controlling my breathing as people pushed against me from all sides until I got to Liv. She had already finished one of her drinks and put the empty cup under her half-full one to free one hand. I grabbed it and spun her around into me. Her mouth parted in surprise, but she glared at me.

"We can't talk here, it's too loud," she yelled, her eyes now dancing with amusement.

I leaned into her and put my lips against her ear. "I'm not here to talk," I said loudly enough for her to hear. Goosebumps rose on her arms, and I slid my hand around her waist to pull her closer. The music pumped, but I barely heard it. All I could feel were my hands on Liv's waist, and the way her eyes locked on mine made my heart thrum faster.

Suddenly she pushed away from me and headed to the bar for another drink. I sighed, thinking that maybe I had pushed her too far. I watched helplessly as she led the bartender onto the floor and they started grinding together.

Rage tore through me like a wildfire, scorching every thought in its path. Somewhere in my mind, I knew that she wasn't mine, but right then it felt like she was or had been, and I'd just lost her.

23

OLIVIA

My head was too full of alcohol, frustration, and lust. The way Lucas had been dancing with me had sent my heart into overdrive, and I had surprised myself as much as him when I pushed him away.

I'd needed to get my bearings and put some space between us. I hated the way my body and emotions betrayed me by wanting him so badly. Didn't my feelings realize how much I'd been hurt? This night needed to end.

It was petty to grab the bartender to dance with me, but I had to get away from Lucas. The proximity to him was dangerous, and I was too drunk to protect myself.

The bartender's moves were rougher than Lucas's. Had I kissed him that night a few weeks ago? I couldn't remember.

My intuition was screaming at me that I should have stopped drinking several drinks ago, but instead I took another long pull of my Sex on the Beach and let the alcohol numb me some more. It didn't matter how much chemistry Lucas and I had; he had a whole damn family he hadn't bothered telling me about, and I just couldn't forgive him for that.

I'd picked that particular club figuring the cute bartender would be there. But dancing with him wasn't having the effect

I'd hoped for. Instead of forgetting all about Lucas, I was even more aware of his presence. I moved the bartender's hands off my butt, again, and he still pulled me closer.

Looking around to see if I could spot Mela, I found Lucas's blazing eyes inches from my face instead.

He spoke into my ear, causing more goosebumps to appear on my arms. "You should go home; you've had a lot to drink."

"I'm good," I called as I patted his chest like I was dismissing him.

He grabbed my hand and held it there. Bartender guy tried to pull me from his grasp.

"I'm serious, Liv. You're not being safe right now. You should really go home," Lucas said it more loudly this time, making my cheeks flush.

The bartender shoved Lucas and raised his voice. "She's fine, man. You need to back off."

Lucas's eyes hardened. He was struggling to contain his anger. "You don't want to touch me again."

The testosterone in the air was strangling me, so I touched their chests as I stood between them like a referee. "Lucas, you should go. I know this guy, okay? I'm here with him. You don't have to worry about me, not anymore."

His expression was pained, but I didn't have time to dwell on it because the bartender was spinning me around and away from Lucas. When we finally stopped moving, an angry Mela grabbed my arm.

"What are you doing?" she yelled at me, incredulity written all over her face.

"It's fine, I know him." My words were slurred.

I followed Mela's eyes; Lucas stood by the bar, shaking his head. *Oh, like I'm the one who should be apologizing?* Had everyone forgotten why I was so mad? Memories of the blonde, blue eyed Casey holding *his* son swam around in my brain. Wearing a towel on her head as though she and Lucas had just showered together, before he ran off to get his perfect little family a treat. Tears filled my eyes as I angrily brushed them away.

"Wanna get out of here?" the bartender yelled into my ear, making it ring.

I looked up at him and felt my head nodding. I wasn't going to sleep with him—but that didn't mean I couldn't let Lucas think it. He deserved to feel as crappy as I did.

The bartender didn't waste any time pulling me off the dance floor and dragging me towards the door, where Mela was waiting, somehow having left the dance floor ahead of me. Again, she grabbed my arm and pulled me off to the side.

"You're going home with him?" she demanded with a look of disgust.

"So, what if I am?" I hated how petulant I sounded.

"You're acting like a total bitch, Liv," she said in a low voice.

"*Excuse* me? I'm single, Mela, in case you've forgotten. I can do what I want."

Nate chose that moment to interrupt us, and I could have kissed him for it. He was always so great at diffusing the tension.

"Mela's right, Liv," he said.

"W-What?" I was starting to feel sick.

"You're acting like a child, and we all know this is meant to hurt Lucas. Congratulations, your plan worked. I never thought you were spiteful...until now."

My mouth fell open with shock. Nate had never spoken to me like that in all the years I'd known him. I glared at them both, tears pooling in my eyes again. Turning away from the weight of their judgment, I strode out the door and into the waiting cab with the bartender.

As we pulled away, I glanced out the window and saw Lucas staring after us with such a grief-stricken expression that my heart, once merely cracked, broke completely. It felt like it would never be fixed again.

24

OLIVIA

"Just let me out here," I mumbled to the cab driver, a kind Hispanic man in his late fifties.

"This isn't my place, babe," said the bartender—whose name I still didn't know. His dark eyebrows creased in confusion.

"I'm not your babe, and I'm *not* going home with you. Please let me out here."

I was grateful when the driver pulled over. Tossing a twenty at the bartender to cover my ride, I stumbled out of the car and onto the sidewalk.

The bartender's eyes blazed at me, but I didn't care. He rolled down the window to say something, but mercifully the driver drove away before I could hear what it was. I could guess what he'd been about to say; it likely had to do with me wasting his night.

Stumbling down the sidewalk, I moved in a familiar direction. Before, I had been drunk and careless, and now I just felt like an idiot. In my mind, I kept seeing Lucas's face, crumpled with grief and pain. A sob escaped my lips. *Why the hell did I do that to him?*

Feeling like a piece of crap, I dug out my phone and called my sister.

"Liv? It's almost midnight. What's going on?" Amanda pressed.

I tried to say something but instead I burst into tears and wailed into the phone.

"Liv! Oh my gosh. Are you hurt?" She sounded panicked.

It felt like I was hyperventilating as I tried to catch my breath. "Not...physically," I managed to sob into the phone.

"Oh, sweetie. Where are you?"

"I'm walking up to Mom and Dad's driveway. Can you sneak me into your room?" I sniffed.

I'd had the good sense to get dropped off near my parents' place, knowing that Amanda was still there. Why I felt led to cry on *her* shoulder, of all people, I had no idea, but I went with it anyway. Maybe I wanted to feel that good old Christian judgment I so richly deserved.

A few minutes later, I was sitting in her room downstairs, having snuck into my parents' house. It was the height of irony that I used to sneak out of their place and now I was sneaking in to avoid them, but I wasn't feeling up to laughing.

I sat cross-legged on her bed, clutching a small throw pillow and rubbing my hand over her soft purple duvet. Looking around the room, I saw that my mother had turned it into some kind of craft space. A table against the wall was littered with scraps of material for sewing and boxes were piled high in every available corner. Clearly, they hadn't anticipated Amanda's return, or mine. There was hardly space for the bed.

She grabbed a handful of tissues and thrust them into my lap. I took one and wiped at the tears still steadily streaming down my face. It was pointless since they just kept coming, but it made me feel like I was at least doing something about it.

"What's going on, Liv?" Amanda whispered. There was no trace of anything but concern in her voice. I knew that would change once I was honest with her, and somehow I looked forward to being properly shamed.

After opening and closing my mouth a few times, I realized that I had no idea where to start or how much I should tell her. "I don't want to be like this anymore," I finally said. Tears continued to stream down my face.

Amanda reached over and grabbed my hand. "Like what?"

Looking down at the bed, I mumbled, "I hurt people—on purpose. I push them away and make sure they can't get too close. No matter what I do I feel lost—anchorless, really."

"How long have you been feeling this way?" she asked gently.

"I want to say since G.G. died, but I know that's not the truth. The truth is that this has been growing inside of me forever, but it's gotten worse ever since Lucas left three years ago. I threw myself into running and made it my entire identity, but then I lost that dream and…I guess I lost myself too." My shoulders slumped under the weight of my epiphany as my tears continued.

"Why do you think it got worse when he left?"

I stared at the bits of fabric on the table. All mismatched and purposeless—kind of like me. "After the court case, I wrote him a letter and told him I loved him. I thought that it would be enough for him to stay, and when he didn't and didn't even bother to write back or anything, I think a part of me shut down. If that's how it went when I opened up and let someone in, then I didn't want to do it again, I guess."

As I said the words, I realized they were true. Being rejected by Lucas had caused a deep chasm of pain I didn't want to face, so I never let guys get close enough to hurt me. *As if that's helped.*

"Oh, Liv. What happened tonight? I'm guessing something pretty major?" Amanda asked.

Here is where I knew that she'd have no choice but to judge my actions. Deep down inside, a small ember of hope was being lit by the kindness of her tone, but it couldn't last.

"I've been drinking a lot, Amanda. Like…a lot. Basically, every night I'm either out at a club drinking and dancing, or I'm getting drunk alone in my apartment just to dull the emptiness. I let random guys kiss me and put their hands on me and I make them think I'll sleep with them, but I never do."

My hand continued to rub the soft duvet as though I was absorbing its softness. Back and forth, back and forth, as I let the words I'd been avoiding fall out of my mouth. I told her about Lucas's son and how I found out. About how he'd been trying to talk to me for weeks and I kept shutting him down. And about how much I still loved him despite everything.

"Tonight I felt like he was getting too close to me, so I pushed him away and made him think I left to sleep with the bartender. He looked so hurt, Amanda. I've never seen anyone look at me that way before. And Mela and Nate, they were so disappointed in me. I just…I don't know if I can come back from this."

I choked on a sob, and she patted her lap for me to rest my head in it, the way she'd done when we were little and I had a booboo.

She let me cry for a long time, not saying anything, simply holding me and rubbing my back as I wept. Eventually my tears subsided, but I kept my head in her lap anyway.

"Can I ask you something?"

"Okay," I croaked.

"Do you *want* to keep going down this path?" Again, there was no judgment in her words, and it was much more than I deserved.

"No," I groaned. Not wanting to go down the same path and actually getting off it were two very different things, though. I wasn't sure I knew how to change directions after so long.

"Then maybe it's time you tried something new." The inflection of her voice on the last word made it sound like a question.

I supposed it was my choice, whether to try something else. Everything I'd done was a total failure, and I was miserable. My best friends were disgusted by my actions, and I'd hurt the boy I loved so deeply that I wasn't sure he'd ever forgive me.

"Like what?" I asked.

"Why don't you come to church with me? Experience something new, meet different people. A lot of people your age are there. If you keep doing the same thing expecting a different result, you'll go insane. That's the literal definition of the word. So, why not try something else?"

I thought about Lucas's face once more. How pained his expression had been. How disappointed both Mela and Nate had looked when I left with the bartender. More than anything, I wanted to be a better person; I just wasn't sure how to.

Lucas had shown kindness to me since he'd gotten back, and I'd thrown it in his face. Yes, he had kept his son from me, but maybe there was more to the story.

Church was the last place where I thought I'd end up, but if my sister was this non-judgmental, maybe the people there would be too.

"Okay, I'll go," I whispered.

She sighed, with relief I thought, and for the first time in a long while, I felt some semblance of peace.

25

LUCAS

Just let me go.

Maybe I should have just let her go when she sent me that text. It certainly would have made my life a lot easier. Instead, I watched her leave with the bartender and I went home to my empty apartment.

Even though I'd gotten to work early today, my productivity sucked. I slammed the hammer on the nail in the two-by-four right at the edge making the wood crack—again. *Dammit.*

It was a dreary and rainy day, which matched my mood perfectly. The roof had recently been placed on the house we were building, so at least we were dry. I wasn't sure whether the hardhat made my head pound or if it was the rage within me. Or maybe it was just the hammering and sawing all around.

There was a sizable crew at the site, getting things ready for the next phase of construction. I had been useless all day, too preoccupied with Liv and thoughts of that bartender's hands all over her.

I glanced around to see if anyone had noticed my mishap with the wood and caught the look of curiosity on my boss's face as he watched me from across the room. I shrugged a little sheepishly and tensed as he started walking over.

"Hey, Derek."

"You do know that we have a nail gun for this?" He looked at the discarded pile of wood quickly rising beside me.

"Yeah, sorry, I uh, wanted to hit something today," I confessed.

"I noticed. Want to talk about it?" he offered.

I wanted to say no, but holding it all in would cause an even worse eruption. Then again, he was my boss.

As if understanding the conflict on my face, he said, "How about for the next ten minutes I'm just your friend and not your boss?"

With relief, I word-vomited the events of the weekend, telling him about trying to talk to Liv and having to watch her leave with someone else.

"Ouch. Why didn't she want to talk to you in the first place?" The tone of his question made me wonder if he suspected that there was more to the story.

"Well, I kind of didn't tell her I had a kid because I'd literally just found out about him and hadn't figured out how to do it. But then she found out from my ex, and Liv thinks I'm still with her."

"Ah. So what did she say when you told her you guys weren't together?"

"I...hadn't gotten around to telling her yet."

"I had a feeling." He smiled sympathetically. "It can be challenging to speak to women at times. Heck, I've been married for a decade and I still struggle to communicate with my wife on occasion. Can I give you some advice though?"

"I'll take whatever I can get, man," I said with a rueful laugh.

"When you're in the doghouse, always lead with the most important information first because it might be the only chance you get."

"What do you mean exactly?"

"I'm willing to bet that when she walked into the dinner party you said something like, 'We need to talk.' Am I right?"

A little defensively, I jutted out my chin—but when I met his gaze, there was only softness in it. "Yeah, that's exactly what I said, actually."

"Had you started with, 'I'm not involved with anyone, please let me explain,' she might have heard you out. That's all I meant. Get to the root of the issue as quickly as humanly possible. Telling her you needed to talk may have translated in her mind to you trying to explain why you were in a relationship when the crucial piece of information was that you aren't in one at all."

He was right, but none of that changed what she had done. Going home with him? It was unforgivable. "I'll try to keep that in mind next time," I said biting back my sarcasm.

"You might consider forgiving her too," he said as he studied my face.

"And why exactly would I do that?" The rage that had subsided while we talked was now making a vengeful comeback.

Derek seemed to weigh the words he was about to speak. The sun was coming out and rays poured into the newly installed window above his head. The thought of just letting this all go and acting like it had never happened made me want to throw something through the window.

"Look, I get it. Forgiveness is one of those sticky subjects, especially coming from a Christian because it's been used to sweep a lot of heinous things under the proverbial rug. Does she deserve to be forgiven? No, not really. She hurt you—seemingly on purpose—and that's not easy to let go," he started.

He picked up a piece of split wood from my pile and then reached over to grab the hammer I'd set down on one of the construction tables. Carefully, he pulled the nail out of the wood.

"You know the anger that's about to boil over within you right now?" he asked.

I nodded, too angry to form any kind of coherent sentence that wouldn't jeopardize my employment.

"That kind of anger eats away at a person. Eventually, it

causes that person to lash out, and what happens then is like what's happened to the wood here. The nail is out, sure, but the damage has been done. Things said and done in anger can't just be taken back and erased as though they never happened. When you hold on to un-forgiveness, that anger has nowhere to go because you've bottled it up. On the other hand, when you choose to forgive, all you're really doing is choosing to let go of the anger and hurt that's causing you way more problems than it'll ever fix."

Slowly, I massaged the tension out of my hands, then gave him a measured look. "Isn't that just letting someone off the hook for hurting you though?"

"It doesn't have to be. If someone did something to you that was illegal, you could forgive them and yet have them convicted under the full extent of the law. One does not negate the other." He shrugged and then went on. "To be honest, I've always found forgiveness to be kind of a selfish act. I'm letting go of the anger so that it no longer consumes me, but that doesn't mean there won't be any justice. In a case like this with you and her, that's a little different. I imagine you still care for her, though you also want to pretend you've never met her."

I couldn't help but wince at his words. He likely knew as well as I did that I would never want to erase Liv's existence from my mind, but I understood what he was saying.

"What the hell do I do then?"

He looked at his watch quickly. "Oh, careful there, you're almost out of friend time. I'll be turning back into your boss in about thirty seconds." I laughed as he went on. "You still care about her, and if you want any chance of ever moving beyond this, then you'll have to do it without the anger overshadowing every thought, every conversation, every action… You'll need to remember how much you care about her, and that's going to be next to impossible if you're still pissed. So, my advice? Let it go so you can move on. But what do I really know? I'm just your boss."

He clapped me on the back of the shoulder as he walked back to the blueprint of the house and gave some direction to one of the crew members.

The day had started in a rage, and now I wasn't sure what I felt. The hurt hadn't disappeared, but a willingness to consider forgiving her began to take shape. And maybe that's what Derek had been talking about. I could admit that it was much easier to think when I wasn't fueled by a burning desire for revenge or violence.

At the end of the day, as I was packing my gear into my car, I saw Derek a few cars over and waved at him to say goodbye but also thanks. He nodded with understanding. Although I was still unsure of what to do, at least my feelings were more in control. For a Christian, he was surprisingly chill about me having a kid out of wedlock, too. I'd thought they were pretty against that sort of thing, but he hadn't even batted an eye.

I sighed when I pulled into the parking lot of my building, knowing that I had a long night of journaling ahead of me. It was the only way I was going to be able to sort through the mess in my head, and I knew it.

26

OLIVIA

We walked into the church, and the first thing I noticed was the ceilings and the massive windows, like those of a cathedral, lining either side of the building. Light streamed in and landed on the theater-style chairs locked together in sets of twenty. I knew because I counted them—at least the ones in the middle rows. There was probably enough seating for a thousand people, with a second and third level.

My stomach fluttered as we walked deeper into the sanctuary and were greeted by a woman who looked to be in her mid-thirties.

"Amanda, it's so nice to see you," she said with a smile. "And who's this with you?"

"Marilyn, hi. This is my sister, Olivia. She's never been to church before," Amanda said.

The woman, Marilyn, gave me such a kind smile that warmth spread right through me. She grasped my hands, looked me in the eye, and said, "You are most welcome here, Olivia."

I lost the ability to speak for a minute but smiled. She let me go and ushered us in, and I followed Amanda to some open seats near the front. Instruments were on the stage, but no one was playing them yet. We took our seats as more people filed in, smiling and greeting each other like long-lost friends being reunited once again. It all felt so…happy.

A timer on the screens above and beside the stage were counting down the last few seconds—to what, I wasn't sure, but I nervously anticipated what was next. The moment the timer finished, the lights in the sanctuary dimmed, and spotlights fell on the stage, where a handful of people who looked around my age walked over to the instruments and began getting ready.

A girl about my age stood behind a keyboard and started to play some hauntingly beautiful notes. A guy a few years older grabbed one of the guitars and slung it over his shoulder to strum along with the keyboard. Another young guy with darker skin and black hair sat at the drums awkwardly looking around like it was his first time playing in front of a crowd. He was behind what appeared to be a cage of plastic panels. A young woman stood at a microphone in the middle of the stage and started speaking.

"Hello, everyone! My name is Tessa, and if this is your first time to Gateway Church, I just want to welcome you here. We're gonna get things started with some worship and then the message from Pastor Dan. If you would all stand with me…" She gestured with her hands for us to stand, and a chorus of chairs flipping up could be heard around the room.

The music started playing and I became lost in it. Such achingly beautiful songs about loss and hope, and a savior who loved everyone. It was like being at a concert with colored spotlights, electric guitars, and the most beautiful harmonizing I'd ever heard. Men and women alike seemed to connect to the music, and hands were raised through the sanctuary, as though people couldn't help themselves.

After a good twenty minutes, the pastor came onto the stage and started preaching. He spoke of forgiveness and making things right with the people we'd hurt. It felt like his message was especially for me. He was animated and passionate, and it felt like he was drawing on his own experiences, which made me feel less alone.

"No matter what you've done in your life, there is nothing that is beyond the hope of Jesus. There is nothing you can't come back from. There is nothing and no one that can't be forgiven," he said.

Even me?

He had us bow our heads as he prayed, and music began pouring out of the keyboard once more, adding to the emotion of the moment.

As he finished his prayer, he said, "If anyone here is feeling lost or alone, like all hope is gone...I invite you to give your heart to Jesus. He is waiting for you. He loves you. He wants a relationship with you, no matter what you've done, and he is ready to fill that hole in your heart that nothing else seems to fill. All you need to do is come up to the front, and we'll pray for you and show you how to do it."

The music started again as people began trickling to the front of the room to be prayed for. Tears streamed down my face as I listened closely to the lyrics of the song. It spoke of a savior who didn't care what you had done; he would go to the ends of the earth to find you because you mattered. *Could that really be true?* I wondered.

Amanda slid her hand in mine, and there, in a room full of strangers, I felt like I had finally found a place. The peace that had begun a few nights ago wrapped around me, calming my heart like a balm. I swayed to the music, still holding Amanda's hand, and though I would never be able to explain it, I felt like I had been called there for that exact moment.

To my surprise, my feet carried me to the front of the room, just below the stage, where some knelt in prayer and others wept what seemed to be tears of joy. It was there that someone prayed for me, and as Amanda joined me with tears in her eyes, she led me through a prayer asking Jesus into my heart, and offering to let him lead my life. I'd been doing a terrible job of it anyway, so it felt like a welcome relief to hand that responsibility over to someone else. To someone who loved me beyond reason.

I didn't deserve forgiveness for all the things I had ever done, but somehow it was given to me anyway, simply because I had asked. And at that moment, I realized that I, too, had the power to forgive anyone, and the person I most wanted to forgive and receive forgiveness from was Lucas.

As peace washed over me, it was clear that I needed to make things right with him. That must have been how my sister felt when she realized that she needed to come back to Florida to repair our relationship. Maybe God really did care about all of us in such a powerful way that he would send a woman across the country to fix what was broken and lead her sister onto a better path. Maybe I was supposed to help Lucas in a similar way.

It had only been a couple of minutes, but something deep inside of me understood that everything had just changed. There was a lightness to my soul that hadn't been there a few minutes before, and though I didn't know the words to the song that was playing, I hummed along anyway, feeling as though the music was in me.

I didn't know what would happen next, but I felt a hopeful anticipation bubbling up in my chest. Whatever happened, I knew I would never be the same again.

27

LUCAS

"Hey, Lucas, sorry I'm late. It's been a crazy morning," Casey said as she stepped into my apartment to drop off Luke.

I scooped him up and blew a raspberry on his cheek. He squealed with laughter. Setting him down on the couch with an episode of Paw Patrol I had queued up, I nodded towards the kitchen for Casey to follow me. As soon as we were out of Luke's earshot, I confronted her.

"Why did you send those texts to Liv?"

Several emotions flashed across her face. Shock, frustration, anger, fear, and then defiance.

"She needed to know about Luke. It wasn't fair to him."

Good, she wasn't denying it. "Oh, you were just looking out for him, huh? You expect me to believe that?" My jaw ticked with frustration.

"I'm sorry if it caused problems between you two." She sounded more hopeful than apologetic.

"It was clearly your intention to drive a wedge between us, and I want to know why."

I took a step towards her and her eyes widened with surprise as she stepped back. We stood off in the kitchen until her shoulders slumped in defeat.

She blinked back tears and said, "I'm sorry, Lucas. I love you, okay? I knew that if you just spent enough time with us as a family, you'd realize you loved me too. Olivia would have gotten in the way of that."

It was what I had suspected, but it still shocked me to hear her admit it. "You were trying to drive her away? What did you say to her when she came over that morning?"

She had the good sense to look embarrassed. "I told her that you were out getting a treat for your son." She blew out a breath and added, "And I made it look like we were together by putting a towel on my head like we'd just taken a shower."

Nausea swept through me. No wonder Liv had assumed we were a couple. Casey still looked as though she expected me to profess my love for her any second.

"Casey, I need you to hear me on this. I don't love you and I never have. I'm in love with Liv and I have been for years."

"You'll change your mind, Lucas. I know you will," she said stubbornly. "You'll see that we belong together someday."

Had she heard me at all? "I won't. And if you ever go behind my back like that again, we're going to have some serious issues. Got it?"

"I'm sorry, Lucas. I wasn't thinking," she said after a pause. "You're right, it was unforgivable of me to go behind your back like that. It…it won't happen again." With a sudden sob, she let herself out of the apartment as I stared after her.

"We go out?" Luke's voice broke into my thoughts. He was standing in front of me, tugging on my pants.

"You want to go to the park, bud?"

He nodded and was practically vibrating with excitement. I walked over to the bag Casey had left for him, and my heart sank as I realized there were no sand toys in it. Evidently, I had been relying too much on her and hadn't gotten my own stock of toys for him. It wasn't that big of a deal, but I realized that the whole fatherhood thing still overwhelmed me a bit.

I knelt and helped get his shoes on, knowing I'd likely carry him most of the way, and he wrapped his arms around my neck to steady himself. The tiny action made my heart swell with love for him.

When I opened the door, I nearly fell over. Liv was standing on the other side of it with her fist up, about to knock. Her eyes registered surprise and then something else I didn't recognize. Regret? I wasn't sure. Her hair was in a braid and some loose strands had escaped, and I had to restrain myself from tucking them behind her ear. We stared at each other for a few moments before I realized that she really was standing there.

My jaw fell open as she smiled widely. "Hey." She sounded a little unsure of herself.

"Hey," I said enthusiastically, resisting the urge to rub my eyes and make sure I wasn't dreaming.

She lifted a mesh bag of sand toys. "I thought maybe you guys would want to go to the park?"

At hearing the magic word, Luke started jumping up and down yelling "Park! Park!"

My eyes met Liv's as we laughed, and though I had a million questions for her, we simply walked to the park together in silence. It was just a few minutes away, but it felt much longer because I had no idea what to say. Seeing her at the door, I forgot all about the way she'd gone home with that bartender. The anger I'd been expecting was conveniently absent. All I felt was unadulterated joy as we walked side by side and Liv held Luke's hand seeming to accept him.

Once we got to the park, Liv sat cross legged on the sand and started pulling out the toys. She and Luke began shoveling sand into a castle-shaped bucket and packing it down. Expertly she flipped the bucket upside down, and Luke screamed with delight as a perfect sandcastle appeared before his eyes. I cleared my throat to release the sudden emotion choking it.

They dug a moat together, and Liv poured water from a bottle she'd pulled out of the bag. Luke's mind was blown when she produced a small boat from her pocket and directed him to drop it on the water. He pointed and squealed as it floated. Liv looked at me, as I stood awestruck behind them, and grinned. I couldn't help but grin back at her.

I wondered if it was strange we weren't talking about anything that had happened, but I figured we'd get there eventually. She hadn't said a word about how the night had ended at the club, but she didn't really need to. Her just showing up and being there, prepared to play with Luke, meant a lot to me.

Pulling myself out of the trance I had entered, I sat with them in the sand. I crashed the boat into the side of the moat and made dramatic crashing sounds, expecting Luke to laugh. Instead, he put his hand on my arm firmly and said with a very serious expression, "No. No crash here."

Apparently, that was a game for the apartment. Liv snorted and tried to cover it up with a fake cough. I smirked and apologized to Luke. An hour later, after pushing him in the swing, watching him go down the slide a hundred times, and creating a five-story sandcastle, it was about time to pack it up. I wasn't ready to say goodbye to Liv, though.

"Who wants to go for ice cream?" I asked.

"Me!" Luke and Liv said simultaneously.

We walked to the ice cream parlor, where I took Luke to the washroom to get him cleaned up. Once we were sitting at a table, Liv with a scoop of black cherry, Luke with a scoop of chocolate, and me with a double scoop of cotton candy ice cream, we ate in companionable silence. As soon as Luke finished, he got down and started playing in the ball pit a few feet away. I was highly aware of the fact that it was the first opportunity Liv and I had had to talk without his little listening ears.

"I didn't go home with that bartender, Lucas," Liv said simply.

My heart rate quickened, betraying me with the hope I had refused to entertain. "Why did you change your mind?" She had seemed pretty set on going home with him, and I couldn't help but feel surprised at finding out she hadn't.

Her cheeks reddened. "I, uh, was never going to sleep with him."

"You weren't? Why did you let everyone think you were going to?" What I really meant was why had she let *me* think she was going to, but it felt too vulnerable to admit that.

"I wanted to hurt you, Lucas. And I'm so sorry for that. When I saw your face..." She paused and swallowed hard before going on. "I've never felt so badly about anything before. I felt so awful, actually, that it helped me make some pretty big changes. I'm not drinking anymore and I uh...well, I've started going to church."

Of all the things I thought she might say, that was the last. But I found myself cautiously optimistic for her. "I think that's great, Liv. I'm happy for you. Especially about the drinking. To be honest, I was getting worried."

Glancing over at Luke to make sure he hadn't drowned in the ball pit, I turned back to her.

"Can I tell you what happened that day?" I asked.

She nodded, knowing what day I meant.

"Casey is Luke's mom, and we dated for a few months, long after you and I had broken up. I had no idea that she'd gotten pregnant, and she'd told me about it a couple of weeks before that day. We aren't together, but I guess she wants to be. Luke came over for his first overnight visit and she insisted on spending the night too. I let them have my room and slept on the couch. I left my phone charging in the living room, and she's the one who texted you that day, not me. I was figuring out how to tell you about Luke, and that would never have been how. I didn't even know you'd come over that morning until Mela yelled at me at the dinner party." I lowered my voice to a whisper and added, "I'm so sorry."

She was quiet as I kept my eyes trained on Luke, to make sure he was safe and because I couldn't face her disappointment. Finally, I couldn't take it anymore and glanced at her. Her lips were twitching like she was trying not to laugh.

"What?" I demanded.

"Mela yelled at you?"

"Yeah. She's pretty scary for such a tiny woman…"

Liv's eyes danced with laughter before they grew serious. "I do wish you had told me about him yourself, but I can understand how hard that would have been."

I appreciated the olive branch she was extending more than I could put into words. "Honestly, I thought you wouldn't want to have anything to do with me if you knew I had a kid. And I would have understood, but I guess I wasn't ready to let go of the idea of us yet. It was selfish."

She rested her cheek on her knuckles thoughtfully. Her green eyes stared so deeply into mine, it made my lungs feel like they were being squeezed. "I forgive you, Lucas. Can…can you forgive me?"

I smiled and reached across the table to pull her hand into mine. "Of course."

She looked down at our linked hands. "So…friends?" She laughed.

"Always…"

Liv unlinked our hands and grabbed the mesh bag of toys, sliding it across the table to me. "Here. Nate and Mela mentioned that you've been feeling a little in over your head."

"And you came to help?" I asked, hardly daring to let myself believe that she had come to help me bond with a child I had with another woman. My heart was in serious danger of never getting over her and I knew it.

"I'm pretty good with kids." She shrugged like it was no big deal and glanced at her watch. "I've actually got to get going, but let's hang out again sometime. Okay?" she asked with trepidation, as though I might not want to.

"I'd love to."

She smiled and walked over to Luke, gave him a high five, and waved as she left. I stared after her until she was out of view.

28

OLIVIA

"Olivia, would you like to share your testimony with the group?"

A girl named Makenna had directed her question at me.

I was at my first young adult group in the church, and we were in the pastor's living room, sitting in a circle. Christmas had come and gone, and I'd spent it with my roommate since I was still not speaking to my parents. My sister had gone back out west for an extended visit, and I had continued attending the church she'd brought me to.

There were two couches across from each other and a bunch of folding chairs to make up the rest of the seating. I had grabbed one of the chairs after some giggling girls crammed on the couch together. They smiled at me kindly, and I tried not to feel out of place.

Makenna was one of the pastor's daughters, and I had never seen her looking less than perfect, with manicured fingernails, flawless makeup, and hair that never had a single strand out of place. She was always listening with her head cocked to the side, like a curious bird, and that was how she watched me now. There were about twenty of us in the room, give or take, both guys and girls, and the sound of someone's heels clacking on the hard marble in the kitchen echoed in my head. I flushed as I realized I had no idea what a testimony was, and everyone was watching me expectantly.

"My testimony?" I asked, hoping she would expand on what she meant so I wouldn't have to ask in front of everyone.

"Yeah," she replied—then her eyes widened as she realized I had no idea what she meant. "It's the story of how you came to know Jesus. I'm sorry, I forgot that you were a baby Christian." She laughed.

My face flushed again, but I answered eagerly, hoping that I was among friends. "Yes, it was very recent," I admitted with a small laugh. "I was in a really rough place, actually. I had lost my dream of running after an accident, lost my great-grandmother, was drinking all the time, kissing strangers in bars... I was a mess." I stared at my hands as I spoke. My sister had told me that a lot of people gave their hearts to Jesus after hitting rock bottom, so I figured being honest was the best course of action. Why sugarcoat my story?

"Anyway, my sister had returned to town after moving out west because God told her to come and fix her relationship with me. After a particularly rough night of making some seriously terrible life choices, I went to her and completely fell apart. She was kind, and not judgmental at all. When I went to church a few weeks ago, I was so moved by the service that I went up to the stage for prayer, and my sister led me to Jesus."

I finished speaking and looked around the quiet room shyly.

Eventually, Makenna said, "That's, um, great. A great testimony." She reached over and patted my leg.

Maybe I've overshared, I thought—but the awkwardness of the moment passed quickly as someone else was invited to share. The girl's story wasn't quite as messy as mine; in fact, she had grown up a Christian and given her heart to Jesus as a child. Most of the stories around the circle were similar and it made me happy for them that they hadn't struggled the way I had, although it was hard for me to relate to them.

"Who wants monkey bread?"

Makenna's mother came into the living room wearing a red apron and with what looked like a brown sticky beehive covered in icing that smelled like cinnamon and sugar and deliciousness. The layers pulled apart easily, and I grabbed a small doughy ball when it was offered to me. People were right about church-lady food; it was heavenly.

Laughter echoed around the room, and I overheard snippets of conversations about the latest hockey game, a recent engagement, and a fundraiser coming up. Tessa came and took the chair beside mine. She was the one relaying the announcements before church at Gateway.

"Olivia, right?" she asked.

"Yes."

"What's your story?" Just after asking, she laughed at a joke told across the room.

"My story?"

"Yeah." She waved her hand airily. "Where are you from? Who's your family? That kind of thing."

It felt like a job interview I hadn't prepared for. "Well, I was adopted, and I've lived in Florida for most of my life," I started.

"You were adopted? That's so wonderful! I've always wanted to adopt. It's the right thing to do."

"I mean, it's a little more complicated than that," I started, feeling defensive, for some reason.

"Oh, I bet. I've heard the process can be really challenging sometimes. I'll probably do it someday. I'd love to open my home to a child in need." Her eyes sparkled and got a faraway look in them.

I shifted in my seat, chiding myself for starting the conversation with being adopted. How had I thought it would go?

"Anyway, it's really good to have you here. Let's go for coffee or something sometime," she said breezily, and then hopped up to go chat with someone else.

A few minutes later, the pastor popped into the room to say

hi. "I wanted to make sure you'd all heard about the fundraising campaign going on for our ministry teams. We're looking for any and all ideas to raise money because we have a lofty goal to reach, and I'm not sure a bake sale is going to cut it this time." He chuckled, and others joined in.

My heart leapt as I forgot the awkwardness with Tessa—especially considering it was my fault for bringing up adoption. I had heard the fundraiser mentioned from stage at church, and an idea had been ruminating around in my mind ever since. This seemed to be as good a time as any to bring it up, as he was looking around the room expectantly.

"I have an idea," I said. Everyone looked at me and I gulped before going on. "My job is actually in event planning; several months ago we planned a fair, and it raised a lot of money. We could hold it in the church's parking lot since it's so big, and I could basically plan the whole thing using the design from the last one."

It wasn't like me to speak up that way, but I really wanted to help. The church talked a lot about acts of service, and I figured this could be mine.

The pastor's face broke out into a wide grin. "That sounds incredible…uh—" He looked at me as though willing my name to come to his mind.

"Olivia," I offered.

"Olivia, right. That would be wonderful. Why don't we set up a meeting with the staff and volunteers, and you walk us through what you'll need to make it happen. I imagine there will be permits required and stuff of that nature?" he asked.

"Yes, I have a list of everything that would be needed. I'll just need to check with my boss to make sure that she's okay with me doing this," I said, kicking myself for not having asked Carrie before. She would probably say yes—she was just that kind of person—but I wanted to make sure.

"I'm sure your boss will be fine with it. It's for Jesus, after all. He'll work everything out," the pastor said kindly.

I nodded in agreement.

A WEEK LATER, Carrie had given me permission and I had met with the church and a team of volunteers. It was decided that I would head up the project with the pastor's two daughters, Makenna and Faith. The young adults would help.

I was brimming with excitement at putting my skills as an event planner to use for such a great cause. It felt almost like the reason I had gotten the job in the first place was so I could help out now, when it was needed most.

A few structures would need to be built, and I sent a message to Lucas to see if he'd be willing to help. He wrote back quickly saying he'd love to, and we made plans to meet at the church the next day since it was a Saturday. All in all, things were going well, and for the first time in a while, I felt truly happy and fulfilled.

29

LUCAS

"Lucas, hey!"

As Liv called to me, I was pulling Luke out of his car seat. She jogged across the parking lot to us. It felt almost like she was running in slow motion; she looked hot in just an everyday outfit. I smiled as she leaned down and gave Luke a high five.

"Follow me to the p.a.r.k." She spelled it out so Luke wouldn't start running.

We rounded the corner, and as soon as he saw it, he screamed and did start running. I chuckled as we moved closer so we could watch him and talk about the plan.

It was a surprise when I got her text asking for help with such a big project. I hadn't seen her in action before, and this was a new side of her I was excited to discover. We sat down on a bench in front of the park while Luke ran around with a couple of other kids who were there with their moms.

"Okay, so what's the plan?" I asked as I kept an eye on Luke.

"Right, so basically we're going to run a fair in the parking lot here in about eight weeks," she started.

"A whole fair? Like with rides and everything?" I asked, impressed.

"Yes! I ran one a few months ago, and it was a huge success. We'll work with a pop-up carnival company that will set up a bunch of rides, and we'll sell things like candy apples and cotton candy, have food vendors volunteer to sell food, have games set up like ring toss, stuff like that. It's going to be so great," she said as she kicked her feet excitedly.

I'd never seen her like this before, and it was captivating. "That sounds amazing. So, where do I fit in? How can I help?"

"Well, I know you're just a few months into your new construction job, but I was hoping you could help build a few of the structures for things like ring toss and a selfie booth."

"A selfie booth?"

"Yeah, it's basically just an oversized structure with a giant picture frame decorated with the date and the name of the fair where people can take selfies. We can make one for friends and one for couples. It's essentially just a way for them to take pictures and remember how much fun they had. Do you think you could build those?" she asked uncertainly.

"I'm sure I can figure it out," I replied, assuming it couldn't be that hard.

The look of relief and joy on her face was worth it. "Thank you so much, Lucas. It'll be so nice having someone on the team I kind of know." She laughed with a tinge of uneasiness.

"Are you nervous?" I prodded.

She bit her lip, making me want to lean over and kiss her.

"I'm terrified. On the one hand, I know I can do this; I've literally done it. But on the other hand, it's a lot of pressure, and I want to make a good impression, ya know?" Her eyebrows crinkled with worry.

I wanted to fix the problem, but did not know how to.

"You'll be great, I know it. And I'll be here to help." I reached over and put my hand over hers, feeling a jolt of electricity between us. I wondered if she felt it too.

My phone started ringing in my pocket and I reluctantly let

her go and pulled it out. The caller ID showed that it was Casey, so I excused myself to answer it.

"What's up, Casey?"

"Where are you? I need to pick Luke up. His doctor just called and has an opening today. I wanted his ears to be checked and his appointment was weeks away, so I want to take advantage of this." The sound of a horn in the background let me know she was already moving.

I glanced over at Liv, who was watching Luke argue with the kids he'd been playing with. "I'll just meet you at my place. I can be there in twenty minutes."

"That's not fast enough. I'm already driving, just tell me where you are and I'll get him."

I gave her the church's address and hung up. I didn't want her anywhere near Liv, but I couldn't very well refuse to let her pick up Luke.

Turning back to the bench, I was surprised to see that Liv wasn't on it. I looked around and found her marching over to Luke, who was now sitting on the sand in tears, looking like he'd been pushed.

"Pushing isn't nice," Liv told one of the boys as she raised Luke by the hand and brushed the sand off him. Luke picked up a handful of sand, and before I could stop him, he'd thrown it at the boy's face.

Crap. The boy's mom stormed over and grabbed her now shrieking son. Liv apologized profusely as I bent to scold Luke for throwing sand.

We walked back to the parking lot, away from the screaming, so I could grab his things from my car.

"Everything okay?" Liv asked.

"Yeah. It's just that Casey needs to come get Luke for a doctor's appointment." I ran my hand through my hair.

Her eyes widened. "She's coming *here*?"

"Yeah, I'm really sorry. I tried to meet her at my place, but she's in too much of a rush."

Liv looked at me pensively. "It's fine. But you'll understand if I don't stay and chat?"

I laughed. "Of course."

A few minutes later, Casey came flying into the parking lot. I strapped Luke into his car seat.

"Thanks for this, Lucas. I can drop him back to your place in a couple of hours," she offered.

My eyes were on Liv, who was talking to a few women by the church doors.

"Just text me when he's done, and I'll let you know if I'm still here or not," I answered.

Casey's gaze had followed mine and was now on Liv. "You've introduced our son to her?" She said the word 'her' like a curse word.

I glanced at Luke as I closed the back door. "Yeah, why wouldn't I? He's met Nate and my brother too, which you didn't have a problem with," I reminded her.

"They're not your girlfriend," she seethed.

"Liv isn't my girlfriend, Casey. You kind of saw to that, remember? So, yes, I introduced Luke to my *friend*."

She huffed and opened the driver's door to get in. "I'll text you when we're done."

I didn't like the way her eyes narrowed at Liv. As I walked back, I wondered how I would protect her from whatever Casey was planning.

30

OLIVIA

We were only four weeks out until the fundraising fair, and things were going smoothly. I couldn't help but be impressed with my own organizational skills.

Lucas and I were at the church, decorating some of the props he had built, and all I could think about was how much he'd helped me over the last few weeks, and how effortless it was to be in his presence. It was a simple kind of thing, but I couldn't seem to take my eyes off him.

"I can feel you staring at me, you know," he teased without looking at me.

I flushed and laughed out loud at the inside joke we'd shared so many years before. We were outside painting the props at a picnic table. I stretched, leaned back on my elbows and turned my face up towards the sun. It was a little chilly but not too bad, and I loved the warmth on my skin.

Lucas stood to stretch as well, and his hoodie rode up to show his toned stomach. My eyes darted away, but my heart had been sent fluttering.

Standing up quickly, I started walking back to the church. "I'm going to go inside and get some more paint," I called.

His mouth turned up into my favorite lopsided grin, and I had to stop myself from going back and hugging him just to feel his arms around me again. It was getting harder to stay in the just-friends territory.

In the sanctuary, a group of volunteers were working on the signs we'd put up around the city. The pastor's wife, Lucinda, walked over to where I was gathering paints to take outside.

"Olivia, hello. You've done such a wonderful job of bringing this all together. I'm very impressed," she said kindly.

I smiled back at her. "I'm just so happy to help."

She looked past me out the window, at Lucas. "Who is that guy out there?"

"That's my friend Lucas," I said quickly, not wanting to get into an explanation of our past.

"Ah, I see. He has a child, yes?" She asked in an innocent tone, but warning bells went off in the back of my mind.

"He does."

"Is he married?" She looked at me expectantly.

"No."

The beige dress she had on made a swooshing sound as she tapped her foot. "Hmm," she said.

I gathered the paints in my arms and moved to leave, but she put a hand on my arm to stop me.

"Some of the women have been a little concerned that you're spending so much time with a man who has a child out of wedlock. And I heard he threw sand at Missy's toddler?" Her brown eyes stared at me as I tried to control my reaction.

Was this 1950? Were the ladies in the church really gossiping about me spending time with an unmarried man who happened to have a child? And why had she even asked me, if she already knew the answer? Noting the look on my face, she backtracked a little.

"It's just that as Christians we need to be very careful about how our actions may be perceived by others. We are constant representatives of Christ, you know," she said.

"Didn't Jesus hang out with prostitutes?" The words were out before I'd had a chance to consider them. I nearly threw my hand over my mouth in shock. *Real nice, Liv.*

Lucinda's face reddened and her eyes narrowed so slightly I might not have noticed it, had I not been looking for her reaction. "There's no need to get defensive, sweetheart. I'm just trying to look out for you," she said while rubbing my arm.

"Of course. I'm sorry, I don't even know where that came from."

Excusing myself, I left the sanctuary and made my way back to Lucas. I might have been a "baby Christian," as Makenna had put it, but I was pretty sure Jesus wouldn't have been judgmental about people's pasts. Making a mental note to be careful who I confided in at the church, I walked over to Lucas just as Casey showed up to drop Luke off.

Lovely. This day keeps getting better and better. She definitely wasn't my favorite person.

"I didn't think you had Luke today?" I asked him as she started unbuckling the boy from his car seat.

"I wasn't supposed to, but she asked if I'd mind because something came up last minute. Is it okay that he's here?" His expression was full of concern.

"Of course, it's no problem. I was just surprised to see Casey here again," I said quietly, not wanting her to overhear.

"She does seem to have a knack for needing my help when I'm with you, doesn't she?" It seemed that he was beginning to get a little suspicious of her.

Casey walked over to us, and I could see that Luke had some kind of liquid all over his chest.

"Luke just spilled his juice, I'm so sorry." She handed Lucas a bag. "He has a full change of clothes in here. You may want to do it now if you're staying out here; it's kind of cold."

She bent down to kiss her son and headed back to her car without a word to me. Not that I minded.

Lucas sighed. "I'll be right back, okay? I'll just take him to the washroom inside."

He scooped up his son and jogged him into the church, much to Luke's delight. The sounds of the boy's laughter carried to me and made me smile.

"Uh, Liv, right?"

I cringed as I heard Casey's voice behind me. Slowly I turned and she was in her car with the window rolled down, a few feet away. I considered ignoring her but remembered Lucinda saying we were representatives of Christ. Guilt had my feet moving towards Casey.

"Yes?" My tone was passive.

"I know you don't like me," she started.

Very astute.

"But I can see that this whole church thing seems to mean a lot to you."

"Yeah, it does," I said, unease building in my stomach. Where was she going with this? Had she spilled juice all over her son so that she'd be able to talk to me alone? Maybe I was being paranoid.

"I just wondered how your church friends would react to knowing that Lucas is a former convict." She said it with such sweet concern in her voice that if I hadn't known she was out to sabotage any chance he and I had of getting back together, I might have believed her sincerity.

"What are you talking about?" I sighed with frustration.

"You didn't know?" Her eyes widened with mock innocence. "Where did you think he went for two years? An extended vacation?"

She laughed. I didn't.

Suddenly, everything clicked into place. His disappearing act, the silent treatment, the way he blew back into town with no warning and wouldn't tell anyone where he'd been.

"Casey!" Lucas's tone was sharp, and it made us both flinch. He stood on the other side of the gravel road.

Casey's mouth lifted into the tiniest smirk before she covered it up with an innocent expression. "See ya later," she called to me as she drove away, leaving a cloud of dust to settle between me and Lucas.

I whispered a quiet prayer to myself. "Jesus, I think I'm gonna need your help with this one."

31

LUCAS

Sometimes you can look back at your life and say, "There, that's the moment I wish I could take back."

For me, that was it. I stood there, helpless, as Casey drove away knowing that she had probably told Liv the one thing I'd never wanted her to know.

I searched her face for some sign that she might forgive me—again—but her expression was unreadable. Slowly I walked towards her while still holding Luke. The day had gotten considerably warmer, but I felt chilled to the bone.

Why hadn't I just told her I'd gone to prison? She smiled cautiously, and a spark of hope ignited in me. Maybe Casey hadn't told her what I'd assumed.

"What did she say to you?"

She opened her mouth to speak but seemed to think better of it. Shaking her head at me with a sorrowful expression, she nodded towards the park and I trailed behind her. When Luke was happily going up and down the slide and we were sitting on the bench, she finally spoke, staring straight ahead.

"Lucas, I want you to trust me enough to tell me the truth about your past."

It seemed easy enough, but how could I explain that it wasn't so much a matter of trust but an overwhelming feeling of unworthiness? I had gone to prison. I could never be who she wanted or needed with a past like that.

Taking a deep breath, I leaned forward and rested my elbows on my knees while I told her about my biggest shame.

"After the court case, I spiraled pretty hard. I had already been circling the drain, but then I pretty much hit rock bottom. I was drinking all the time, smoking a lot of pot, and then I drove to Massachusetts and met some guys I really hit it off with. We started hanging out, and they let me move in with them. They always had a ton of money lying around, literal stacks of cash piled up around their apartment. They offered to let me in on what they were doing, and I stupidly agreed."

Luke had found a shovel and pail and was building a sandcastle by himself. I watched as he scooped sand into the bucket until it was full and then slammed it upside down on the sand like Liv had taught him. He was the picture of life and innocence. It made my heart ache.

Liv put her hand on my arm and squeezed it encouragingly without saying a word.

"They were stealing ATM machines full of cash. I joined in and we started hitting a few each week. We'd do a smash and grab, go somewhere secluded to break into it and take all the money out. Then we'd split it evenly between the three of us."

Putting my head in my hands, I allowed the shame to consume me. I really was trash. I'd always known it.

"Then what happened?" she asked.

"The cops got tipped off and one of the guys got caught. I got away, but in exchange for a lighter sentence, that guy ratted us out, so we both went to prison too. We didn't hurt anyone physically or anything. It wasn't a violent crime, but it was still a crime, and I spent two years behind bars."

The weight of my confession made me feel I was being smothered the longer the silence stretched between us.

"Why didn't you just tell me, Lucas?"

I risked a glance at her and was surprised to see her eyes soften. "I didn't think you'd want to have anything to do with me if you knew. It's not something I'm proud of. After the way I treated you during the trial, I was shocked when you found me and gave me that letter. And I kept it. I must have read it a thousand times."

"Then why didn't you stay? Or write me back at least?"

"I was no good for you. I'm still no good for you, but I'm trying to be a better man. One who deserves you. A part of me thought I was protecting you from me and another part was afraid of letting you back in. I'm so sorry, Liv." I choked on the words and again buried my face in my hands.

"Hey," she called softly and put her hands on my face. Her green eyes held mine, and I found myself unable to look away. "Thank you for trusting me. I can't imagine how hard it's been to carry this secret, or how much shame you've felt. None of this changes our friendship. I don't care what you've done in your past, Lucas. I know who you are."

She pressed her hand to the spot right over my heart and a sob escaped my lips.

Could she really be so understanding about something like this? Her eyes flickered momentarily to my lips as she leaned in and pressed hers against mine for just a moment. Sparks of electricity shot through me as my emotions warred against each other. Sadness, grief, joy and lust swirled through me.

She pressed her forehead to mine, still holding my face. It felt like the most intimate moment of my life.

Liv let her hands drop and folded them in her lap. "I want you to know that I would never judge you for something like that. We all have skeletons in our closet, and we've all done things we wish we could take back. I assume you're not still stealing ATM machines?"

"No, ma'am. I'm on the straight and narrow now." I bumped her leg with mine, making her laugh.

"That's all that matters in the end, really. We can't go back and change our past. All we can do is move forward and make better choices. You're doing exactly that, Lucas. You have nothing to be ashamed of."

She smiled, stood up, and walked over to push Luke in the swing.

I stared after her in a daze. I didn't deserve her grace, but I was grateful for it. As I watched her push my giggling son higher and higher in the swing, I fell even more in love with her.

A new resolve arose in me to become the kind of man who deserved her and could make her happy. We were still just friends, but I hoped that someday we would be much, much more.

32

OLIVIA

"This is amazing, Liv. You really pulled it off."

Lucas squeezed my hand affectionately. The church parking lot had been turned into a full-fledged fair. It was packed with hundreds of attendees who had bought tickets and were spending money on games, food, and rides. I didn't need a calculator to know that we were going to surpass our fundraising goal.

I'd been there all day and felt exhausted but thrilled. It was getting dark out, but the flood lights we'd erected kept everything bright. The structures Lucas had built were all decorated and adorned with twinkle lights, which gave everything a fairy-tale vibe. We'd sold out nearly every kind of food the members of the church had made, and the vendors all had big smiles on their faces. The lines had hardly stopped all day. I took a moment to just bask in the successful event I had orchestrated.

Mela and Nate appeared in the distance and walked towards us arm in arm.

"You came!" I called out, running to Mela and flinging my arms around her neck.

"Of course we did. You knew we weren't gonna fight forever.

Besides, I couldn't handle getting one more 'I'm so sorry please forgive me' text from you," she said with a playful shove.

"I really am sorry about that night," I said.

"It's in the past. Water under the bridge. And any other cliche you need to believe that we're good, m'kay?" she said with a laugh.

"Okay, okay." I laughed along with her while Nate and Lucas chatted.

"Seriously, though, this looks like Coney Island or something," she marveled as she pointed to the rides and games.

It did look fantastic. People from the church had been coming up to me all day to tell me what a great job I had done. I felt so indescribably happy.

Mela and Nate went off to explore before things wrapped up, and Lucas went with them. Out of the corner of my eye, I saw the pastor get onto a stage we had put up for announcements and start to corral some of the volunteers. He tapped the microphone, and those within a twenty-feet radius who could hear him made our way over to the stage.

"This has been such an incredible event," he started, and the crowd that had gathered cheered loudly. "There are a couple of key people that I want to highlight and thank tonight." He paused for what felt like dramatic effect.

I imagined being called up to the stage to receive accolades. Part of me was glad my friends weren't there to see it, and another part was disappointed. I couldn't deny it was nice to be publicly praised.

"There are two people here who were instrumental in planning and executing this event. I'd like to ask my daughters Makenna and Faith to come up here for a minute."

Confusion swept through me as I watched his daughters join him on the stage, not looking nearly as surprised as I felt.

"You ladies did such an amazing job organizing all the volunteers from your young adults group. It was definitely a team effort, but you led the charge and are responsible for the church's most successful fundraising event ever. Can we give these ladies a round of applause?" He started clapping and everyone else followed suit as I stood frozen in shock.

They had barely done anything to help. I didn't understand why they were getting all the credit for the event I'd worked my butt off to make happen for their church.

Tessa came over and stood beside me. "Good job on this, Olivia," she said.

"Uh, thanks," I replied faintly.

"What's wrong?" she asked, cocking her head to the side.

She and I weren't close, but I did consider her a friend.

"Well, I mean, I planned this whole thing, and Pastor Dan didn't even mention me or anything," I said, trying not to sound like a whiny brat.

"Is that why you did this? For the praise?" Her tone was gentle, yet I felt my defenses rising.

"No, of course not. But Makenna and Faith hardly did anything to help. I guess I'm just surprised they got all the credit…" I trailed off.

She looked at me with a mixture of pity and sadness. "It sounds like you're struggling with some pride, Olivia. You clearly *did* want to get the credit for this event, when honestly Jesus should be the only one getting the credit. Pride is not the Christian way. You may want to spend some time in prayer about this." She patted my arm in a way that felt just a little bit condescending.

Did that seriously just happen?

Later, as the fair wrapped up and we were starting to clean up, the pastor called for all the volunteers to gather around for a picture. Reluctantly I started to walk towards them when I felt someone pull my arm. When I turned, I was surprised to see that it was the pastor's wife, Lucinda.

"Olivia, may I speak with you?" she asked.

"Now?" I gestured to where everyone was lining up for the picture.

"Yes, now." She pulled me away. Her lips were pursed as she looked me over as though considering me.

"Olivia, we're going to have you sit out of the picture this time," she started.

"What? Why?" I demanded.

"It's just that the picture will be going out to the church bulletin, and we're very selective about who gets to be seen as a prominent member of the church. The thing is, you have some repenting to do, and it can't be done while you're consorting with unmarried members of the opposite sex."

"Wh-what?" I stammered.

"To be honest, it can't be done while you're spending time with *any* man. You really need to get right with Jesus first, and then you'll be seen as a member of our church." She patted my arm in the same condescending way Tessa had, and my face flushed with humiliation as she walked over to the group to pose with them.

Shame threatened to suffocate me; I choked on the injustice of it all. I wanted to scream, and cry, and bury my feelings in a giant vat of ice cream. As I turned to walk away, the humiliation intensified as I caught sight of Lucas standing a mere few feet away. Judging by the look on his face, he had heard every damning word.

Kill me now.

33

LUCAS

I left Nate and Mela as they walked to their car and headed back to find Liv. Maybe I could help with the cleanup.

Truth was, I just wanted to spend some more time with her, and if I had to clean up a fair while doing it, so be it. I smiled as I thought of how happy she'd looked all day. It was nice to see her in her element again—something I hadn't witnessed since she'd competed at that track meet.

She was talking to a woman who looked familiar, but I couldn't quite place her. A group of volunteers we'd worked with for the last several weeks were posing together for pictures. As if in slow motion, I gazed at them and back at Liv, who was standing so still she looked frozen. A sinking feeling started to build in the pit of my stomach, and I moved closer to hear what the woman was saying to her with that patronizing look on her face.

"The thing is, you have some repenting to do and it can't be done while you're consorting with unmarried members of the opposite sex," the woman said.

Blood rushed to my head and I saw red as she went on about how Liv needed to get right with Jesus before she could be "seen" as a member of the church. *Consorting with unmarried men.*

She made Liv sound like a whore. Even from the side, I could see Liv's face crumple under the woman's words. My jaw was clenched so tightly I thought it might shatter under the pressure.

The woman walked over to the group to pose with them, smiling as though she hadn't just devastated the woman I loved. Liv turned towards me and the look on her face made me want to hurt someone very, very badly. Her eyes widened as she saw me standing there, and she cringed as she realized I was close enough to overhear their conversation.

"Liv," I said, trying to keep the rage out of my voice.

An array of emotions flickered across her face. For a moment, there was pure vulnerability in her eyes. She shook her head slightly and reined in her feelings one by one until there was only indifference left.

"Lucas, hey," she said, sounding devoid of any emotion. I could practically see each brick she had just placed in front of her heart in protection.

"She doesn't know what she's talking about," I started, but Liv waved dismissively, as though it hadn't bothered her.

Her laugh was a bitter sound in my ears, lacking her usual lightness. "It's fine. I have a lot to learn, I guess." I tried to catch her eye, but she wouldn't look at me. "You can go, Lucas. I'll just see you later, okay?"

She didn't wait for me to respond; just like that, I was dismissed as she turned and started picking up some items left behind by fair goers. I backed away, frustrated at having to leave her there with those people.

NOT WANTING to go back to my apartment just yet, I made my way to the beach and let the anger take over. I stomped through the sand and whipped rocks into the crashing waves as I agonized over how to help.

Knowing that Christians were judgmental and seeing them in action were two different things. Until then I'd never had a front row seat to such a holier-than-thou attitude. It made me wonder how anyone ever found faith at all.

I stood still and listened to the sound of the waves crash against the shore to calm myself down. The truth was, Liv's newfound faith had had positive effects on her. She'd stopped drinking, was making better choices, and the light that had gone out in her was coming back to life. Or at least it had been, before she was basically accused of prostitution.

I couldn't stop seeing Liv's face—so full of shame and regret, as though *she* was the one who had done something wrong.

Sitting down on the sand, I wondered what made people so callous and cold. Especially people who claimed to love Jesus. A strangled groan escaped my lips as I threw another rock into the waves. If that was what loving Jesus looked like, then I never wanted any part of it.

The looks and raised eyebrows as I'd helped Liv with the structures for the fair hadn't been discreet. No one had talked to me in all the weeks I'd spent there. Evidently, they'd just been judging me the entire time and coming to their own conclusions about us. I hadn't wanted to discourage her when she was trying so hard to embrace her faith and make friends with people who supposedly shared it, so I'd never mentioned any of it.

Shouldn't faith be easier than that? After tonight, there was no way I could keep sitting back and watching her get hurt. She had been through enough. The accident, losing G.G., Ali trying to stop her from going to the funeral—and I was pretty sure she wasn't talking to her adoptive parents. What she needed was a win, not another loss—but loss was what they had just given her.

But reflecting on Christianity made me remember something—or someone. I pulled out my phone and winced at the hour, yet that didn't stop me from finding a number and dialing.

The call connected, and I wasted no time.

"Hey, sorry to call so late. I need a favor."

34

OLIVIA

It was Sunday morning and I was in sweats, wallowing on my couch. I couldn't bring myself to go to church, knowing they'd be recapping the amazing fair. I couldn't listen to the pastor praise his daughters for all the work they hadn't done.

Maybe it had been silly of me to expect I'd make friends there easily with a past like mine. They'd all grown up in the church, and I was basically a harlot to them, for all intents and purposes.

Flipping through Netflix, trying to find something to distract me, wasn't working. Heat flooded my face as I remembered how Lucas had heard everything Lucinda said to me about him. I pressed one of my roommate's decorative pillows into my face and screamed into it as loudly as I could. That actually did make me feel slightly better.

Pulling out my phone, I hovered over my sister's number, debating whether to tell her what had happened. She'd feel awful and maybe even blame herself, and I didn't want that.

Instead, I went into my room to grab the Bible she had gifted me before she left. If I wasn't going to go to church, I could at least spend time reading about what I was supposed to believe in.

As I flipped through the pages of the Bible, the words became impossible to read as tears blurred them. *It's not really a surprise is it, Liv? You've always struggled to belong anywhere. Why did you think this would be any different?*

I closed the Bible and pulled my knees into my chest, hugging them and putting my head down. Taking a deep cleansing breath, I counted to four, envisioning an imaginary square in my mind. Inhale in—one, two, three, four—the square was drawn. I held the breath for another four seconds as I drew the square again, then let my breath out for four final seconds as I traced the invisible square once more. It was a coping strategy I'd learned from therapy after my accident.

I was just trying to put the hurt back inside by turning my focus to something else, but I didn't care. If Christians really were like that, then maybe I had dodged a bullet.

A half-empty bottle of vodka on the TV unit caught my eye. For a moment, I missed the numbness that alcohol brought. My old life had certainly had its share of complications and regretful mornings, but at least I'd known where I stood.

A knock at the door brought me out of my own head, but I considered not answering it. Who would it even be on a Sunday morning? The mystery visitor was persistent and knocked again, so I got up, sniffling, and peered through the peephole.

It was Lucas. I jumped back and started frantically wiping my nose and patting down my hair. Glancing in the mirror, I made a face at my appearance: glassy red eyes, splotchy face, bird's nest on top of my head. There was no way he wouldn't realize I was wallowing.

"Come on, Liv. I know you're in there," he called from the hallway.

I opened the door cautiously. He took one look at me and his expression changed to one I didn't recognize. He leaned against the side of the door, since I was still blocking the entrance, and smiled.

"I'm not really up for company, Lucas," I mumbled, looking down at the ground.

"That's all right, I'm not staying," he said easily.

"Okay, then."

"But neither are you," he added as he slid past me and into my apartment.

"What? Have you seen me? I'm not going anywhere," I argued as I folded my arms across my chest.

"Yeah, you might want to change. And possibly wash your face." There was amusement in his eyes.

"And where, pray tell, are we supposedly going?" I asked purely out of curiosity, having no intention of leaving my apartment.

"To church," he replied and moved into the living room.

"Too soon, Lucas."

"I'm not kidding. Go get dressed," he said as he gently pushed me backwards into the hallway towards my room.

"I'm not going anywhere," I said, daring him to argue.

He put his hands on either side of my arms and held my eyes. "Will you trust me? Please?"

The *please* caught me off guard. He looked so earnest, it was challenging to stick to my resolve. But I didn't want to go to church and hear the announcements and see all those people—none of whom had defended me.

On the other hand, Lucas so rarely asked me for anything, and he had been there the night before. He'd know I wouldn't want to go, and yet he was asking, so I figured he had a reason.

I sighed and made my way to my room to get ready.

FIFTEEN MINUTES LATER, I looked much more presentable but still not fantastic. I had thrown on jeans and a long sleeve shirt and put my hair up in a bun because it was way too knotted for anything else. I'd put on just enough makeup to cover up the worst of the blotches and just some clear gloss on my lips. Shoving oversized sunglasses on my face, I followed Lucas out to his car and got into the passenger seat.

He turned on some background music and let me stare out the window in silence as he drove, holding space for me without trying to force me into a conversation. I appreciated it more than he probably knew.

It took me longer than it should have to realize that we weren't going to Gateway. When I looked over at him, he was smiling to himself, focusing on the road and avoiding eye contact.

He pulled into a parking spot and I got out hesitantly after him. He beckoned me to follow him in and I found myself hovering closely behind him, as though he was a shield. The building was older, and above the doors was a sign that said, "Welcome to Sonlight," which I had to admit was a pretty clever play on words. I kept my eyes down, not wanting to meet anyone's gaze.

We walked into a large room with a vaulted ceiling and chairs interconnected with each other. From the corner of my eye, I saw someone wave Lucas over. He waved back and looked at me to make sure I was still with him, then headed over to a man I'd never seen before.

"Derek, hey!" Lucas called when we got closer. Derek leaned in and gave Lucas a one-armed hug, as he was holding a little girl in his other arm.

"Liv, this is my boss, Derek. Derek, this is Liv."

Derek extended his hand to me and grasped it warmly. "Hey, Liv. I've heard so much about you. This is my wife Emily and my daughter Katie," he said as he made the introductions.

"It's so nice to meet you, Liv. And you too, Lucas," Emily said with a laugh.

I smiled shyly. "It's nice to meet you too."

They moved some stuff off two of the chairs next to them. "We saved you some seats," Derek said as he pointed for us to sit down.

I looked at Lucas as we sat down and my heart swelled. His

boss must have been expecting us if he'd saved us seats. It meant that Lucas had arranged for us to be there ahead of time.

He leaned towards me and I breathed him in. "These people are different, Liv. I didn't want you to lose your faith because of some bad examples."

Tears threatened to fall and I looked away. Some friends of Derek and Emily came over and introduced themselves to us. Everyone was kind and welcoming, and despite myself, I felt some semblance of hope beginning to return.

The music started and there were no spotlights or drum cages—simply a young guy with a guitar and a girl on a keyboard. As they sang about love and trust and hope in Jesus, I felt goosebumps rise on my skin from head to toe. The same peace I had felt when I gave my heart to Jesus enveloped me now.

We sat for the service and the pastor came out wearing jeans and a hoodie. He talked about how important it was to come as you were and not worry so much about outside appearances. What mattered was the heart, and that was what Jesus cared about most.

"You can't clean a fish before you catch it, friends. And in the same way, what's the point of going through all the motions of being a Christian if your heart hasn't changed?"

It was beautiful, and exactly what I needed to hear. I relaxed as I slid my hand into Lucas's and pressed my head against his shoulder. Maybe he was right. Maybe some Christians were different.

35

LUCAS

I let myself into my brother's apartment after work with the spare key I hadn't returned yet. The football I'd always played with was somewhere there and I wanted to toss it around with Luke.

As I took in the state of his place, I wanted to kick things out of the way. I was still really pissed about how Liv had been treated by the people at her last church, and even seeing her small smile of hope on Sunday hadn't curbed that fury. I still wanted to march in there and start a fight with the pastor, but I really didn't need assault charges added to my rap sheet.

The curtains were drawn in my brother's place, casting everything into shadows. Clothes and dirty dishes littered the floor and the couch I had slept on for a while. Partially empty bags of chips were thrown around the room as if a wild animal had gotten into them. Old joints were put out in the ashtray on the coffee table and dried out marijuana was carelessly left beside it.

I stomped into the kitchen, where an even bigger disaster was awaiting me. I filled the sink with soapy water, amazed that my brother even had dish soap to begin with, and started furiously scrubbing the dishes and shoving them into the dish rack to dry. Tromping back into the living room, I grabbed the rest of the dirty dishes and loaded as many as would fit into the dishwasher, throwing the rest into the sink to wash.

Once the kitchen was cleaned, my rage fueled me on. I started chucking all the dirty clothes into the laundry hamper and stripped my brother's bed to wash his sheets. If only I'd brought a hazmat suit, I thought to myself wryly. His room was even worse than the rest of the apartment, and I was almost impressed by the low standard my brother had for cleanliness.

As I shoved his DVDs and old books back on his shelf, some polaroids fell to the ground. When I reached down to pick them up, I froze.

There were a dozen pictures of my brother and Casey in *very* friendly positions. Her head on his lap, him kissing her cheek, then one with their tongues down each other's throats.

I dropped the pictures like they had burned me. I knew they'd been friends before I met her, but he'd never mentioned they'd had any kind of relationship. *Why wouldn't he tell me about this?*

A FEW HOURS LATER, I had found my missing football and was sitting on the chair facing the wall when I heard my brother's key in the door. He turned on the light and yelled out in fear.

"What the hell are you doing, Luke?" He gripped his chest as he looked at me warily.

His eyes were bloodshot, and the collared shirt he wore was half untucked from his ragged pants. He stumbled through the apartment as he took in how clean it was. "You cleaned my apartment?"

I couldn't tell if he was happy or furious. I didn't care.

Standing up, I shoved the pictures at him. "What are these about?" My voice was unsteady and filled with anger.

He stared at me for a beat and then his eyes widened as he

registered what he was looking at. "You jealous, brother?" He sneered and tossed the pictures on the coffee table.

"When were these taken, Dyl?" I demanded.

"Who knows? Ages ago, probably." He wouldn't look me in the eye.

I wasn't having it. He had never been great at lying. "Before or after I went to prison?"

His gaze finally met mine. "After. It was after. But we only slept together a couple of times, man; it's really not the big deal you're making it out to be." He tried to laugh it off. "And, honestly, she disappeared after, so whatever," he said with a casual tone, but a flicker of hurt crossed his face before he turned impassive again.

I waited him out. He never could stand silence, and I knew the rest of the story would come out eventually.

Finally, he started pacing across his now clean living room, still avoiding eye contact. "When I found out she had a kid, I sort of panicked, thinking he might be mine. Just to clear my conscience, I had my friend who's a nurse look up the kid's birthdate."

A pit was growing in my stomach. "And did it clear your conscience?" I asked calmly, though I felt anything but.

"Not really, no," he said. "The timing could have lined up with me sleeping with her." He flicked an invisible speck of dust off his shirt.

The pit in my stomach was coming undone and making me feel like I was going to vomit. "What are you talking about?"

Luke had been born in early September, which lined up with Casey and me sleeping together the very last time. And though I had been sure we'd used protection, clearly Luke's existence had disproved that.

My brother looked at me like I'd lost my mind. "When did she tell you he was born?"

"Early September," I replied, realizing how hard she had

tried to get me back. Surely, she wouldn't have lied about me being Luke's father.

"Dude. He was born on October thirtieth," he said almost apologetically.

It felt like I was watching a re-run of the talk shows my mom used to watch. "You are NOT the father." The crowd gasps, chaos ensues. I always wondered why the men even went on those shows to begin with.

But I wasn't one of them. I was still standing in my brother's living room, watching him pace back and forth in front of me.

"You knew?" I asked incredulously.

He glanced at me with a worried expression on his face. "I… suspected. She's never admitted that I was the father or anything. And, clearly, she never wanted *me*."

I heard his words, but I didn't understand them. Had he seriously let me believe that I had a kid for months while he carried on with his life completely unaffected?

"Why didn't you say anything once you saw what was happening?" I demanded.

"Honestly? You seemed to be a natural. When I came over that day and saw you with him, I figured the kid would be better off with you as a dad. At least he'd have a decent one." He shrugged sadly.

The rage made me move so fast he took a step back. "So let me get this straight: You were completely happy to let me take responsibility for *your* kid because he didn't like the way you played with his cars?" The back of my neck was hot, the way it always got when I was about to lose it. "Do you understand how much this has impacted my life? My chances with Liv? You screwed me because you couldn't man up and deal with the mess you made."

"Look, I'm sorry, okay? But honestly, I believed this all worked out for the best in the end. Anyone in my position would have done the same—"

He got cut off as my fist connected with his face.

36

OLIVIA

"You came!" Emily called as she hurried towards me.

She and Derek had invited Lucas and me to their church potluck, and I hadn't decided if I was going or not until that morning. As nice as everyone had been to me, it wasn't easy to forget the acceptance I hadn't received at Gateway. It made me hesitant to open myself again.

In the end, I decided to give it a shot. The ride over with Lucas was awkward and quiet, and I wasn't sure why. Things had seemed so good the weekend before, despite what had happened at the fair, but now he was freezing me out again.

"I did," I told Emily now. "Sorry it was so last minute."

"Don't even worry about it. I'm just glad you're here."

She smiled at me and I was surprised to see that she really meant it, then immediately saddened that I was surprised by someone's genuineness. She did a double take at the look on my face and then put her hands out to help with what I was carrying.

"I made deviled eggs and cheesecake bites. Oh my gosh, I wasn't even thinking. Do Christians eat deviled eggs?" I asked with trepidation.

"Only the chill ones," she said with a wink and a laugh as she popped one into her mouth.

Her eyes sparkled with mischief. I laughed along with her, slightly embarrassed by my panicky outburst.

The potluck was at Derek and Emily's. They lived on a hundred acres, and Derek's company had built the two-story house. It had a large wraparound porch, complete with outdoor ceiling fans and a brick floor, white pillars every few feet and a white tin roof. At least a dozen rocking chairs sat on the porch for guests.

Grass and fields surrounded the property as far as the eye could see, and a pond nestled to the side, reflecting the afternoon sun. A dozen picnic tables had been set up in the grass, and it seemed like most of the church had shown up.

"Your house is gorgeous," I said as Lucas stood stoically beside me.

Concern passed over her face as she glanced at him, but she said nothing. "Thank you so much. Remind me to give you a tour of the inside later." She put her hand to the side of her mouth and stage whispered, "We have kittens."

"Really?" I squeaked out, sounding like an overexcited child.

"Really." She gave me a knowing look, as if she'd known I was a cat person.

"I'll hold you to it," I said as she excused herself to greet some new arrivals.

"Are you okay?" I asked Lucas as I turned to face him.

He was staring at the pond, and that's when I saw that the knuckles on his right hand were torn and bruised. He'd driven with his left hand, so I hadn't noticed it then. He followed my gaze down to his hand.

Shoving it in his pocket, he mumbled, "Yeah, yeah, I'm fine. It's nothing."

I searched his face, but he continued to stare at the water, lost in his own thoughts.

Emily came back and linked her arm in mine to whisk me

away. She wanted me to meet some of her friends. She was probably ten years older than I was, and I found myself wanting to be just like her when I grew up.

"This is Dakota, and this is Cynthia," she said, gesturing to two women sitting at a picnic table. I immediately felt drawn to Dakota's soft gray eyes, and Cynthia's dark, exotic look.

"Hi, I'm Liv," I said as I sat down next to Emily.

"It's so nice to meet you, Liv." Dakota replied. "So, what's your biggest fear?" she asked abruptly, as though it was the most normal question in the world.

"Uh…" I stammered.

"She does this to everyone," Cynthia said with a laugh.

Dakota's open face and Cynthia's small but fond headshake at her friend somehow put me at ease. It wasn't something I'd normally share with strangers, but I found myself blurting out, "Not belonging."

"Ah-h," they said in unison, as if they understood.

"That's a deep one. Mine is abandonment," Dakota said. "My dad abandoned us when I was four, and ever since I've been terrified of people leaving."

My heart ached with sympathy for her. "I'm so sorry."

"My greatest fear is not being good enough," Emily added pensively.

"And mine is trusting others," Cynthia said.

I didn't know what kind of game this was, but I felt a lot less vulnerable after their confessions.

"Why do you think you fear not belonging?" Cynthia asked me, resting her chin on her hand.

This was a very deep conversation for the middle of a potluck, yet it also felt natural. "Well, I was adopted…" I trailed off, not knowing how else to explain. For a moment, I felt like an idiot, remembering how awkward it was when I brought it up to Tessa.

"That'll do it," Emily said as the others nodded.

My mouth fell open. "Wh-what do you mean?"

They gave each other knowing looks, and Cynthia explained. "We all volunteer with a ministry that helps people deal with childhood trauma. Every single adoptee there has struggled with abandonment and belonging issues. I imagine it's difficult to feel like you belong when your biological parents gave you away." Her voice was full of sympathy, but not in a way that made me feel pitied. More in a way that made me feel understood.

Who are these women?

"Wow. I kind of thought that Christians felt it was their duty to adopt all the babies or something," I said, and covered my slightly bitter tone with a laugh. It was certainly how Tessa had made it seem. My eyes flew up to their faces; I hoped I hadn't offended them.

"Adoption is a tricky one," Dakota continued, as if she were really thinking about it. "Obviously, on one hand we as Christians should be there to help and offer a loving home if and when possible…"

Emily jumped in. "The thing is, we're not totally convinced that adoption is the solution. Why not support the birth parents? Why not take them in and help them raise their baby instead of taking it away?"

"You guys seem to have put a lot of thought into this." I couldn't hide the shock in my voice. They were saying exactly what I'd been thinking for years.

"Well," Cynthia said. "When you see the same thing over and over again, eventually you've got to be willing to admit that maybe the solution isn't working as well as everyone thought. I've been volunteering for about eight years, and I've prayed with dozens of adoptees who all had similar wounds. That can't be a coincidence."

"I've actually never really talked to other adoptees before," I admitted.

"There are tons of adoptee only groups on social media. You should look them up," Dakota offered without a hint of judgment in her tone.

They made difficult things seem easy to talk about, and before long we were laughing like we'd been friends for years. I caught sight of Lucas sitting with Derek; they were having what looked like an intense conversation. I hoped that he was sharing his burdens with Derek even if he wouldn't share them with me. It was disappointing that he was still keeping secrets from me. Eventually, I would have to decide if just a friendship would be enough. We would not be able to have anything else if he kept shutting me out the way he did.

Emily and Cynthia ran inside to get more drinks, insisting that I should not help this time because I was a guest—but also threatening that next time I'd be treated like a servant.

I turned to Dakota. "Can I ask you something?"

"Of course."

"Why do you ask strangers what their biggest fear is? No one has ever started a conversation with me that way before."

She laughed easily and said, "Because it's the fastest way to break through the Christian facade of perfection. Too many people who claim to love Jesus try to appear as though they're perfect. As if that's such a possible goal anyway." She snorted. "There was only ever one perfect person, and they hung him on a cross. If I can get someone to admit to a vulnerability right off the bat, then we can really get somewhere. I don't do small talk; I don't do surface pleasantries. And, admittedly, I turn a lot of people off. But, on the other hand, the ones who *are* willing to share—they become some of my favorite people." She gave me a wink and I smiled, realizing I felt the same way.

37

LUCAS

"Listen, after what you told me the other night, I don't blame you for being protective..."

Derek had sat next to me and seen that I was watching Liv, trying to make sure she was okay at a picnic table with several women she didn't know. As usual, he was perceptive.

"I wish I could say I was surprised, but truthfully, I'm not," he continued. "I've been a Christian for a long time and I've seen some...stuff. I'll just leave it at that."

The sound of Liv's laughter travelled to us and I smiled. Or at least I thought I'd smiled, until I saw the look on Derek's face and realized it must have been more of a grimace.

"I'm surprised you came. I didn't think you were into all this Jesus stuff." He waved his hand around at the people from his church.

"I'm not," I said quickly. "But she is, and I'll be damned if I'm going to watch her lose one more thing she cares about."

"What else is going on, Lucas?" he asked after a moment.

It was obvious he knew I was hiding something, but I deflected. "It's nothing."

"Then why do you look like you're carrying the weight of the world on your shoulders?"

"I'm sorry about that. Don't mean to bum out your potluck. I got some…uh, unexpected news last night, and I'm still processing."

"Do you want to talk about it?"

"Not really," I said, then added, "But I guess I should before I blow up and lose my job or something." My tone was meant to be lighthearted, but instead it was raw.

Derek simply nodded for me to go on.

"It turns out my son isn't actually my son." It was the first time I'd said it out loud and the fury that came over me nearly jolted me out of my seat.

"She lied?" he asked incredulously.

"Not only her. The kid is my brother's." I had to stop myself from picking furiously at a scab on my knuckle. "It's like some kind of daytime soap opera."

He blew out a breath. "Oof, that is messy. I'm so sorry. Was your brother's face at the other end of why your hand looks like that?"

"I can neither confirm nor deny that assumption," I said.

Derek didn't laugh; I guess he wouldn't let me off the hook when I used flippancy to confess I had hit my brother.

"What do you think you're gonna do?" he asked.

"I honestly don't know," I said in a more sober tone. "All I feel is anger, and I don't know what to do with it. I want my brother and my ex to hurt as much as I do right now. They allowed me to love a child as if he were mine."

"It's not bad, though, that you love Luke?"

"No!" I said immediately. The thought gave me pause and I almost touched my own heart, where the little boy had come to live. Still. "I started to love him like a dad and I'm not his dad. I made that space, whereas my brother just shrugged off his responsibility. Casey let me believe that because she wanted something for her. Now I'm thinking… I'm thinking that poor little Luke was born to two selfish, lying pieces of—"

I stopped right as a little girl's head emerged on the other side of the table, her big eyes staring right at me. When I looked back at her, she turned and ran. Did I look like an angry monster?

This time, Derek did laugh. "You have developed the instinct to detect when you shouldn't finish certain sentences." He tilted his head at me when I glanced over at Liv again. "How does she factor into what you're saying? Won't she be glad—"

"No!" I cried again. He blinked and I calmed myself before continuing, "She was given away by her biological parents."

"Oh." A look of understanding dawned on his face.

"And she cares for Luke now. To hear that his own mother would lie about his birth, or that my brother would let her…as if this adorable little boy was a piece they could move around in some game…"

Now I rapped the table with my knuckles; I guess I needed the pain, and it was Derek who winced.

Finally, I managed to add, "Liv has been through so much, and I don't know how to tell her this. She is getting herself together, and I can see that going to church has made her a better person. More honest, more understanding, more forgiving. Maybe I'm hoping some of her faith will rub off on me."

"I don't necessarily know about faith rubbing off on someone," Derek said thoughtfully. He wasn't one to BS, which is why I trusted him. "But I do know of some really helpful teachings I listened to when I was fresh out of prison and wanted to kill everyone in sight. They really helped me. I'd be happy to pass them on to you if you want to listen."

There was no pressure in his kind eyes, only the earnest desire to help.

"Sure, if you give them to me, I'll listen." I added a shrug so as not to commit too much, though I knew he would not expect me to. "Maybe they'll help me sort through my thoughts."

"All right," he said, seeing that Emily was trying to catch his attention from the porch. "I need to go cut some meat or I will hear about it. But, Lucas," he said as he got up, giving me a pat on the shoulder, "come clean to Liv sooner rather than later. You guys can face things together. You did that for her by bringing her here, and you should understand she wants to do it for you too."

Yeah, I thought as he walked away and I found Liv's eyes on me. They were sad, which made me sad. *Yeah, she will help me.*

When I pulled up to Liv's apartment to drop her off, I cut off the engine and she kept her hand on the door without opening it, simply waiting. I needed to just say it.

"Liv, I found out last night that Luke isn't my son. He's my brother's kid and they lied to me." I got it all out before I could change my mind.

"Oh, Lucas!" she said.

Her eyes quickly filled with tears, and I realized I would not be able to keep talking about it. In fact, I cursed myself for having said anything.

You should not delay suffering, Derek or some wise person might have told me. But I had always hated seeing her sad more than anything—especially when I or my messes were the cause.

"I can't talk about it right now. I just needed you to know," I added, staring ahead.

"Okay, Lucas. I understand."

She had seen the "Stop" sign, and she spoke with a mixture of sadness and resignation, but I could not even deal with my own emotions at that moment. It was easier to say we should face things together and much harder to start—when all I wanted was for her to be happy.

Liv didn't wait or try to change my mind. Perhaps she was tired of my dramas; she got out of the car, and I didn't want to look at her before I drove away.

YET, over the next week, I listened to the audios Derek had lent me every night while I journaled my thoughts. It was a series of sermons, so it took me all week to get through them, but the more I listened, the more the pastor's words resonated with me.

I sat holed up in my apartment alone night after night, ignoring Casey's texts, writing and listening and writing some more. The sermons talked about the love that Jesus freely gave to anyone who asked, which sounded nice in theory, but he probably meant people without a criminal history and constant fury in their hearts.

On the eighth day, all the sermons done, I put my shoes on and went for a walk. As soon as I stepped outside, the phone buzzed in my pocket and I glanced at it to see it was another apology text from Casey. I deleted it without reading it—again.

I wanted nothing to do with her, ever. I only wanted to see Luke, but I didn't yet know how.

The evening air was crisp and cool as the sun dipped lower in the sky, casting a glow on everything around me. Shoving my hands into my pockets, I walked without a destination in mind and was surprised to find myself at the park where I'd taken Luke so many times.

The memory of him sent a pang through my chest. Guilt had been churning my gut all week at the way I'd pounded my brother's face. Though I kept trying to convince myself that he deserved it, I still felt a strange and overwhelming urge to apologize to him.

In the distance, a father tossed a football with his son. Tears boiled in my eyes as I considered how my own dad had never tossed a football with me, though I'd ended up playing the game for years.

But Dylan had. The thought was a memory I'd tried to repress.

The sun disappeared, and the sky turned pink and orange. Another day had come and gone, and much as I tried, I couldn't keep my thoughts from wandering to the way Dylan had stepped up when I was a child, taking me to and from football practice, coming to my games, helping me train. He'd been the one to show me how to throw a football in the first place. But then he'd grown up and left us behind just like our dad had.

When I started walking again, I had a direction in mind. We couldn't keep repeating the same pattern, and the only person I could control was myself. I couldn't force my brother to step up and embrace fatherhood, but I could still be there for Luke as his uncle, since I was that.

The only way for the abandonment to stop in our family was for someone to stay.

Moving faster now, I thought about how sad my brother had looked when Luke didn't want to play with him, and I was struck with an overwhelming love for both. All they needed was a bridge to each other, and maybe I could play that part. What I needed to do was help, not judge.

But first, I had to apologize.

38

LUCAS

I walked into the club my brother managed and was directed to the back after asking where he was. When I arrived, I spotted him hunched over his desk, poring over what looked like bills. His eyebrows were knitted together like they always did when he was stressed. I winced when I saw his eye, which had turned yellow and green over the last week, and the scrapes on his face.

Standing in the hallway outside his office, I could watch him without his knowledge. He looked exhausted in faded jeans and a jacket over his black t-shirt. He ran his hands through his hair just like I did, which made me smile at the familial trait. I knocked on the door.

He looked up and shock flitted across his face when he saw me. He flinched when I stepped closer, and I raised my hands to indicate that I wasn't armed and was coming in peace. He eyed me warily as I sank down into the chair across from him.

"What are you doing here?" He sighed as though he wasn't up for round two of our fight.

"I came to apologize," I replied.

His eyes narrowed slightly and he searched my face, as if

waiting for the punchline. "You came to apologize," he repeated in a flat voice.

"I did. I shouldn't have hit you and I'm sorry," I said.

"You're *sorry*?" he asked with outrage pointing to himself. "Look at my face, Luke! You mangled it like a damn savage. I should press charges."

"You're right."

Dylan had not been prepared for that. "What's with you?" he asked carefully.

I shrugged. "I don't want any more anger between us, Dyl."

He scoffed with a tinge of anger, but also of hopelessness. "What more do you expect from a family like ours? It's all dysfunction and lies and whatever."

"It doesn't have to be that way, though."

He had been looking for a cigarette inside a crumpled pack, but he stopped at this.

"What you did wasn't okay," I continued, "but we need to be good to each other. We're family. Only you know where I come from, and only I know for you. That matters, you know."

Having fished a bent cigarette from the pack, he started to pull on it to make it straight. He was still listening.

"Dad left and that sucks—"

"Worse if he had stayed, I guarantee," Dylan said quickly and with conviction. His look at me out of his bruised eye made me think he had probably nursed a few of those as a child, and I hadn't. Maybe because of him.

But he frowned against my realization and moved his head away to light the cigarette, blowing the smoke into a corner.

And I had a great desire to leave, so great I gripped both arms of my chair as if I was about to stand up. His eye was quick to see that too, and the same relief washed over his face to think that we were going to leave things unsaid.

Not this time. I put my hands in my lap and stayed where I was.

"It doesn't have to define us," I said, and I suddenly felt all the conviction in the world. "We can do better, man. We have to do better than—"

"Than what?" he said, a smile stretching the cut on his lip. "That legacy of rainbows and unicorns we got?"

My mouth twitched. "Damn, man."

We both began to laugh. Yeah, he knew me, and I knew him. I even knew he was a liar, and I still loved him. And he knew I was violent and impatient, and he loved me.

"Honestly, Dyl, Luke is a great kid."

My brother looked almost alarmed at the sudden change of subject. What did he think we had been talking about all along? Like me, he probably wanted to pretend he didn't know. But he was smoking and listening.

"He's funny and charming and genuinely fun to hang out with. You see the potential with kids, you know? He could truly grow up to be anything, astronaut or football player or"—I thought of Paw Patrol—"cop..."

"Hell, no," Dylan said, horrified.

"Race car driver," I added with a shrug. "He can be anything, *if* he has good men in his life. His dad and uncle."

Hope lit up my brother's face for a moment before despair took its place. "I don't know, man. I wouldn't even know how to start being a dad, never mind a decent one."

"You do know, Dyl. That's just it, you did it for me..."

"Nah, man," he said.

I leaned forward. "You did, and you would have done more if you could. It's not going to be easy. Nothing worth it ever is, right? But do you remember that old movie we used to watch when we were really little? About the guys raising a baby?"

He smirked then answered, "*Three Men and a Baby.* Seriously?" He snorted. "And who is the third man, Nate?"

"We do have another brother you know. I'm just saying. We can do this if we do it together. I'm all in, Dyl. What do you say?"

As if mulling it over, he took puffs of his cigarette, and I had to accept it when the big bit of ash he had neglected to flick on the ashtray fell on his shirt. "Shit, man. I can't fuck this up," he said, more to himself than to me.

"No, you can't." I added, "But you won't."

I didn't wait anymore. I got up and started to go around to his side of the desk. He fumbled with the cigarette as he also stood up, and I saw the fear and happiness on his face when I pulled him into a hug.

We stood like that for a moment, and he grew hot with emotion. He clapped my back hard, wanting me to let go and wanting me not to.

"I'm in, brother," he said against my shoulder in a small but sure voice.

39

OLIVIA

The birds kept singing at the arrival of spring outside my window. It was a beautiful April day, and a gentle breeze rustled my curtains.

I needed to get up soon and get ready for church, but I had a few more minutes to enjoy the tranquility. It wasn't just a normal Sunday: I had been asked to share my testimony with everyone that morning, and I had hesitated, as I did the other times.

It had only been three weeks since I'd first gone there with Lucas, but after chatting with Emily, I realized that if what I said helped even one person, then it would be worth it.

I pulled myself out of bed, took a shower, and put on the turquoise dress I had worn to Mela's engagement party. The dark circles below my eyes were gone and needed no concealer. My eyes sparkled with life, no longer flat and dull. My cheeks, which had recently been gaunt from neglect and borderline alcoholism, had filled out. It seemed sobriety had returned me to my normal self, and it made me smile to see it.

On the drive to church, I rehearsed what I was going to say, trying to make sure I remembered everything. It was nerve-racking, standing up on stage and speaking in front of everyone. My heart skipped a beat as I remembered that Lucas would be in the crowd.

I'd hardly seen him since the potluck; I had given him space to process the lies he had been told and his mixed feelings over not being Luke's father. But when I had invited him to come this morning, he said he wouldn't miss it.

Anytime I thought about him, I was overcome with sadness for what he'd been through. A vicious curve ball, the existence of a child, had been thrown at him, and he'd risen to the occasion so gracefully. To find out it had all been a lie…

As I pulled into the church parking lot, I reflected that it still hurt that he wasn't willing to open up to me, but I couldn't force him. Maybe he'd let me in when he was ready.

Twenty minutes later, I stood on the stage, having been introduced by the pastor. Emily, Dakota, and Cynthia had given me a pep talk and prayed with me beforehand, but now it was just me and a microphone, and my hands shook so much I wanted to hide them.

Lucas sat in the second row with Derek and Emily, and I drew strength from his presence, the same way I had during the court case. He nodded me on just like he had that day.

"I've been through a lot the past few years," I began. "I lost my dream of running professionally after an accident during a race and afterwards I kind of shut down. Alcohol became my crutch to numb the pain, and then I lost my great-grandmother and with her part of myself."

I took a slow breath, giving myself a moment to push back the tears that always came when I thought of G.G.

"When I hit rock bottom," I continued, "my sister was there to help me pick up the pieces. She led me to a relationship with Jesus, and I thought that everything would fall into place after that—and life would be perfect."

I smiled as people around the room chuckled at my naivety.

"What I found was that my hope can't be dependent on other people. Christians are human and imperfect, and there are bound to be kind and unkind ones. There are bad churches that don't reflect the love of God well, and there are great churches—like this one—that embrace imperfections and don't shy away from them.

"I also found grace in the people around me. Grace in my sister who loved me enough to come back to Florida just to fix our relationship, grace in the people at this new church who embraced me and made me feel like I belonged without having to prove myself in any way."

Emily, Dakota, and Cynthia beamed at me.

"And I've found grace in a love for others." My gaze fell upon Lucas, who smiled crookedly, making my stomach twist. "I didn't expect this rollercoaster ride of emotions over the last few months, but knowing that it brought me here to this place, I'd go through it all again. I found hope and grace when I didn't deserve them, and I am so grateful to be here today and share all this with you."

I stumbled a little on the stairs as I got off the stage. The entire congregation seemed to be clapping for me, and it was surreal and slightly embarrassing, but I was proud of myself for doing it scared—for facing my fears.

40

LUCAS

Liv slid into our row after her speech and sat next to me; I had almost stood and moved to her when she'd stumbled, but now here she was, smiling, happy to have shared her story. My chest felt tight with the feelings she inspired in me, admiration and a love that had been burning for a long time. I knew at this point that love could not be put out.

The pastor continued to talk about grace and redemption, and how they were ours for the taking if only we'd humble ourselves and ask. It sounded simple in theory, but I still wasn't sure redemption was ever going to be within my grasp.

Not for someone like me.

"Redemption is for anyone," the pastor said, apparently replying to my private thought.

Not for a criminal.

"Regardless of what's happened in your past, you are not beyond saving," he went on.

I wouldn't even know where to begin.

"Your first step is coming up to the front of the stage and asking Jesus into your heart," he said.

Seriously? It was like he was having a private conversation with me. I glanced up at the ceiling, almost expecting to see a big bright light, and laughed to myself when there was nothing.

Liv let out a gasp and I didn't understand why until I noticed that I was walking to the front of the room. It hadn't been a conscious decision, but now that I was moving, I felt a complete peace about it. I wanted the peace Derek and Emily had, and that Liv had gained. I wanted the same light in my eyes. I wanted that feeling that I'd survive no matter what I went through because I wouldn't just be relying on myself anymore.

Before I could feel any awkwardness at having walked up to the front alone, Derek was beside me, with his hand on my shoulder and a smile on his face. I grinned back, and then other men from the church surrounded me and made me feel wanted and reassured. They guided me as far as they could, and then the decision to follow Jesus was mine to make—and it was an easy choice. My skin prickled from head to toe, as in confirmation that God was real and there with me—with us.

As the men continued to pray for me and my future, my mind drifted to Liv. She had talked about the grace she'd found in love, and I realized that it was true for me too. I had found grace in loving Liv again and wanting to protect her. It was the change I'd seen in her that had made me believe that I could change too; that redemption was a real possibility for me, and that I didn't have to transform myself into someone else to get it.

It was a gift I'd never be able to repay.

Thinking of the way my anger towards my brother had turned into compassion, I felt hope and clarity spring in me like I'd just hit groundwater. Maybe this was the path that would heal my family and keep a little boy from experiencing the pain of abandonment and dysfunction that my family had barely survived.

There was a higher chance of that now than before.

Liv was beside me, taking my hand into hers. I knelt, and the men were also praying for others who had come forward. Liv's eyes were shining with tears as she gave me a watery smile. Her hand came up and hesitantly patted my shoulder like a friend would, and I had a sudden realization.

She was bracing herself for me to leave again. I could see it in the way she looked at me, like I might disappear. Maybe she thought I wasn't stable or capable enough, but the point was, she didn't expect much from me—and that was my own fault because of all the secrets I'd kept from her.

The last few months, thinking I was Luke's dad, had shown me the happiness that came from dedicating my life to someone else. Seeing how happy Liv was for me, though I'd hurt her so deeply, made me understand that I was ready to embrace the love I had for her.

I knew how much I loved the woman kneeling beside me, but *she* had no idea.

It was time for that to change.

41

OLIVIA

Olivia, I want you to remember that you can still find love and contentment in things and in people, even if they've changed.

I recalled G.G.'s words as I laced up my runners and took off at a light jog. My surgeon had cleared me to run months before, but I hadn't wanted to go for an actual run because it only reminded me of the loss.

As I put one foot in front of the other and pumped my arms gently, a giggle escaped my lips and caught me by surprise. I had forgotten how freeing it felt to just go for a run, and G.G.'s words suddenly made a lot more sense to me. Sure, I'd never run competitively again, but I could still run for enjoyment, which was how it had been for me for a long time. I had simply gotten too focused on the pain and forgotten about the joy.

The palm trees swayed in the breeze and the sounds of people milling about or heading to the beach surrounded me. My mouth watered as the smell of tacos and burgers wafted in the air, but I didn't stop. I simply relished running for the sake of it and learning to embrace the things I used to love, even if they weren't the same anymore—just like G.G. had advised me to.

I smiled up at the sky, believing that she was smiling down

on me. Before I knew it, I was jogging up to Mela's front door and knocking, hoping she was there.

Just as I was about to leave, she flung open the door, buttoning her shirt wrong and frantically trying to smooth down her hair. I cleared my throat and raised my eyebrows at her as she grinned and shrugged apologetically, moving so I could walk by her. Nate waved on his way to the kitchen, looking entirely too happy with himself.

"You okay?" she asked as she flopped beside me on her couch.

"Not as good as you are, apparently." I snickered.

"Were you out for a *run*?" she squealed, taking in my yoga pants and sweaty appearance.

"Yeah, I was. It was time." As our eyes connected, I knew she understood.

"This is big."

"It is. I've been making a lot of changes, and I owe you a real apology for how I've acted—and not just for that night," I started.

She tried to wave me off dismissively, but I kept going.

"I'm serious. I was in a bad place and you tried to help—and instead of accepting it, I pushed you away. It was easier to spiral without an audience and…well, I miss you. We've barely hung out lately, and things just don't feel the same even though you say we're fine. I'm so sorry, Mela. Can you forgive me?"

"Of course, Liv. Honestly, it's felt like I've been losing you for a while now. And I think I was too scared to admit it, so I just acted like everything was fine between us, though it clearly wasn't. I don't want to do life without you—ever, okay?"

Mela was starting to look at the ceiling the way she did when she didn't want to cry. She hated to cry, and I was too happy to do it, so my eyes stayed dry and she quickly moved on.

"Tell me about these changes," she asked.

I told her everything from not drinking anymore to how badly the people at Gateway church had hurt me, and how

Lucas had brought me to Sonlight and I finally felt like I belonged somewhere.

"It's been a wild ride," I concluded.

"And where do all of these changes leave you and Lucas?" Her eyes were full of curiosity and something else I couldn't quite read.

I sighed. "Lucas and I will always be friends. I'm starting to understand that he may never be able to give me the kind of relationship that I want—that I deserve. One with full honesty and no secrets. But I've decided to accept it."

She raised her eyebrows but said nothing. "Honestly, Mel. I'm so happy that he's found his own faith."

She waited and added, "And you're completely in love with him."

For once, my friend's brutal honesty didn't catch me unaware or make me want to duck and cover.

"Yes, I'm completely in love with him," I admitted. "I'd rather stay in his life as his friend than try to force a relationship to work between us. I can't compromise on what's important to me, or I'll resent him, and that's not fair to either of us. I'll just have to find a way to live with being in love with my friend until I can get over it."

She was quiet for a while and then asked, "And where do all these changes leave us? Will you still have room in your life for a non-Christian friend?" She was now looking out the window as though she couldn't bear to meet my eye.

"What? Of course! Are you kidding me right now? We don't need to share the same faith or beliefs to share a sisterhood. You're stuck with me," I said as I threw my arms around her and she laughed.

"Oh, thank God because I will NOT be going to church, except maybe for weddings or funerals. And I still plan to sleep with my very hot fiancé, so I don't want any holier-than-thou judgments from you, m'kay?" Although she seemed to be joking,

I could tell by the look on her face that she was slightly worried that might be the case.

"No, Mela. I've experienced what it feels like to be judged like that, and I'm not interested in ever making someone else feel that way—least of all you."

"Well, then, I'm glad to see that deep down you're still the same girl I've always known and loved."

"I am. Besides, I really don't think that hitting you over the head with a Bible or shoving it down your throat would encourage you in any way."

"Probably not. Besides, there are other things I'd rather have shoved down my—"

I pushed her off the couch and she pulled me down with her. Nate came running into the room to see what all the noise was about, only to find us laughing hysterically on the floor together.

42

OLIVIA

"That's the last of it," I said to myself as I poured the rest of my vodka down the drain and tossed the empty bottle into the recycle bin.

It felt like an ending and a new beginning of sorts. After what I endured at the fair, I had held on to the alcohol in my apartment as a "just in case," but the deeper I got into my faith, the less I wanted a backup plan. This was me making a declaration to myself that I wasn't going back to drinking.

It was Saturday morning, and it had been a long week at work. We were planning a big graduation event with multiple schools, and Carrie was giving me more responsibility—and money—ever since I'd proven that I could run an entire fair. She was keeping me busy in a good way.

A knock at the door startled me; I glanced down at my after-work sweats and grimaced. Someone always seemed to come to the door when I was least prepared for it. I made my way to it and checked the peephole, but no one was there. I opened it slightly and looked up and down the hallway, but again I couldn't see anyone.

Just as I was about to close the door, I looked down and saw a box with a card on top that had my name on it. I picked it up and was taken aback by how heavy it was. My heart rate picked up when I saw that it bore Lucas's handwriting.

Quickly I brought it into the apartment and locked the door behind me. I went straight to my room and sat on my bed with the box eyeing it like it might explode. Finally, I opened the card and read it.

Liv,

I know I've kept a lot of secrets from you over the years, and I think it's time that you knew everything. I've always loved you and have carried you in my heart wherever I've gone. I'm hoping that the contents of this box will prove that to you.

If you still want me after all this, please meet me in the parking lot at Pink Lake tonight at 7. If not, that's okay. We'll always be friends. I guess I just wanted you to know that I want more than friendship with you.

Love, Lucas

My heart fluttered like a hummingbird. With shaking hands, I pulled the lid off the box and saw that it was filled with dozens of journals—all in his handwriting. I picked one up and held it to my chest. He was trusting me with his innermost thoughts, and the depth of that vulnerability wasn't lost on me.

Each journal had a number on the spine, and I decided to start with the first one. As I read the initial entry, my hand flew over my mouth with shock.

I met a girl on the beach today. She is the most beautiful girl I've ever seen, but her eyes were haunted. When we accidentally collided, she looked terrified like I was about to attack her, but then when she smiled at me, I knew I was done for. I've never had such a strong urge to protect a stranger before. I don't know what it means. She didn't give me her number or anything, so I don't know how I'll track her down. Maybe I'll run into her again. I'll run that beach all day every day if I have to until she comes back.

I FLIPPED the page and kept reading.

I saw her again! She was at the beach party I almost didn't go to. We hung out all night and I wanted to kiss her so badly before she left, but I couldn't shake the feeling that she's been through something awful, and I just felt that kissing her wasn't the right move. At least not tonight. But I did hug her and she smelled amazing and she fit so perfectly in my arms. Like she was meant to be there. She's friends with Mela, which made me nervous, but I don't think Mela told her what happened at my mom's place that day, so that's good. I'd like her to get to know me before she finds out where I come from.

A FEW HOURS later I had finished several journals, and I couldn't stop reading. Getting a glimpse of the turmoil in his mind during the time we'd been together and after, I was heartbroken that I'd never known how much he was struggling.

Liv moved to New York. I think it was always her plan to leave this place, and me, behind. It hurts and I wish I could beg her to stay, but I can't. Maybe this is what she needs. Maybe she'll come back to me someday. I'd give anything to make things right with her, but I know it's not what she needs. I'm not what she needs. That's why I had to leave her track meet before I could talk to her. I knew if I did, I'd never be able to let her go. And now she's gone and I'm a mess. Sounds like a damn country song. I'm sure I'll get over her someday.

A TEAR SLID down my cheek. He had seemed so indifferent then. I'd convinced myself he didn't care all that much and knowing he did…well, it hurt.

I'm going to see Liv at the courthouse today. I've been dreading it and looking forward to it for weeks. Dyl says I should blow it off, but I don't think I'm allowed to do that. Besides, I want to be there for her even if I can't be with her. Or even show her that I care. She went off to a fancy school in a different state and I stayed here pining for her like an idiot. I can't be that guy anymore. I won't be. Maybe I should start dating.

My heart squeezed painfully at the thought of him dating, though I already knew he'd dated Casey for a few months. The next journal I picked up was different from the others, and I quickly understood why.

This isn't where I wanted to end up. I guess I can't say it's not where I expected to end up because I've always had a feeling I'd wind up in prison, but actually being here is different. There's no one to blame but myself. I need to stay strong, inside and out, and I've started working out three times a day. It helps that there isn't much else to do in this place other than think. I have a lot of time for that now. It's been a struggle coming to terms with where I am, but I know that I can survive this. I have to. Someday I'll get out of here, and I'll need to make better life choices. I'm not going to dwell on my circumstances anymore. I'm here, I'm not going anywhere for a while. I may as well do what I can to make sure I never end up back here again.

I flew through his prison journals, touched by how often he wrote about me. I'd thought of him every day but never imagined that he'd done the same. Reading through his time in prison was hard—really hard—but it gave me a new appreciation for his resilience and courage.

It was after five, and I had one more journal to read. I'd paused here and there to eat something or to cry. He'd been through so much, and yet he was still the kind boy I'd met on the beach. I opened the last journal.

Apparently, I'm a dad now. And I know that this probably means it's over for good with Liv because I could never saddle her with my responsibilities. But at the same time the more I hang out with Luke, the more I love the kid. His mom is obviously a nut job with ulterior motives, but this kid is something else. Smart as hell, funny, sweet. It's not how I planned to become a father, but since it's here, I may as well make the best of it. Even if it means losing the love of my life.

As I read through the rest of his final journal and saw how tenderhearted he was towards Luke, I couldn't help but love him even more. I came to the last entry and read it with bated breath.

Jesus, I don't know if this is how prayer works. I'm pretty new to the whole faith thing, but if you could help me out with Liv, I'd really appreciate it. I want to be with her, but I also want what's best for her. I hope they're the same. If they aren't, please help me walk away. I can't be the reason she doesn't get the life she deserves. But if by some miracle we could be together, please show me what I need to do to prove my love to her. Uh, thanks? I don't know how to end this.

I LAUGHED through my tears and pressed my lips against his journal. Glancing at the clock, I realized I was running out of time. Frantically I pulled open my drawer and started tossing out all the contents until I found what I was looking for. I sighed with relief as I clasped the starfish necklace back around my neck, then I got dressed and flew out the door.

43

LUCAS

"You were great in there, Lucas. A real natural," Derek said, and clapped me on the back.

I couldn't help the grin that spread across my face. We'd spent several hours volunteering at a prison. Not the one where I'd done time, though; it still felt too soon for that. "Thanks, it was surprisingly...okay," I replied.

He gave a big belly laugh and repeated my words. "Surprisingly okay. Ha! I guess I'll take it," he said with a wink.

I hopped into the passenger seat of his blue truck and buckled myself in as we got waved through security to leave. The sun was getting lower in the sky, and my stomach fluttered with nerves as I glanced at the time.

Derek looked over and smiled. "Are you ready for tonight?"

"I think so." I was pretty sure I had everything I needed to meet Liv at Pink Lake, except for the reassurance that she would show up. I had gotten so much wrong, and I just wasn't convinced that dropping off my journals was enough to prove how much I loved her.

"I'm sure she'll show up," Derek said like he was reading my mind. Or maybe the uncertainty was written all over my face.

"I hope you're right." I couldn't help my mouth from turning down. I didn't want to think about what I'd do or how I'd feel if she didn't show up.

Derek dropped me off at my apartment, and after a quick shower I got into my car and headed to the parking lot. Once there, I glanced around nervously, digging my heel into the gravel while I waited. I wondered if I should have planned some elaborate picnic on the beach, but that just didn't feel like us.

My head whipped up as gravel crunched beneath tires, and my heart beat unsteadily. Liv was driving towards me. Was she there to let me down gently or because she still had feelings for me? The unknown wasn't a space I particularly enjoyed occupying. As she got out of her car, something caught the light and reflected brightly, and I sucked in a breath when I saw that it was the starfish necklace around her neck.

I hope that means what I think it means.

"You showed," I said, my voice thick with emotion.

"You didn't think I would?" she asked teasingly.

"Honestly, I wasn't sure. It really could have gone either way," I chuckled, sounding like a frog to my own ears. *Very attractive.*

"Lucas," she started, but before she could continue, I interrupted her.

"Let's go for a walk; there's something I want to show you," I said.

She nodded as she followed me into the forest. Someone had strung lights up to illuminate the path, and her gasp of delight let me know that she was reacting how I'd hoped.

"Lucas, it's beautiful!" she cried.

I stared at her. "It is, isn't it?"

Her face flushed under my watchful gaze. "I'm really touched that you trusted me with your journals. It was... unexpected."

I reached for her hand, and she let me take it as we continued walking. "Did you read some of them?" I asked nervously. It had been an easy decision to drop them off to her, but now that we were together, I felt exposed.

"I read every word," she whispered.

"You read *every* journal? All of them?" I turned to look at her.

She shrugged. "I'm a fast reader."

"Clearly. Well, now you know everything. And you're here."

"I do, and I am," she said in a tone I couldn't quite read—but then she smiled again, and my heart quickened.

We reached the opening to the lake, and a kaleidoscope of color greeted us. Different lights had been strewn up in the trees all around the lake, with lanterns every few feet. The colors were reflected in the surface of the water, and it looked magical.

I had discovered the lights a few weeks before and had wanted to show her ever since.

"It's so beautiful," she murmured as she let go of my hand and walked closer to the lake.

"Liv," I started, and she turned back to face me. I had planned an entire speech, but as I stood before her, I knew what I needed to say. "I love you. I always have. And I always will."

Her eyes filled with tears, but she stayed silent as I stepped closer to her. I took her starfish necklace between my fingers. She'd kept it all this time, and that meant everything to me.

I kept going. "The reason I gave you all of my journals was so that there wouldn't be any secrets between us, and so you'd know that there's only ever been you."

A tear slid down her cheek and I wiped it away. Glancing over at one of the lanterns, I had a sudden inspiration. I walked over and twisted the plastic circle on top of the lantern, pulling it off.

"I wasn't going to do this. I didn't think I should even ask until I had more money, a house, a ring at least..."

Her mouth fell open and she was openly crying now.

"But the truth is, we can do all of that together," I said. "And I don't want to spend another second without you by my side. I guess what I'm trying to say is…" I held up the plastic circle, but before I could say anything else she cut me off.

"Yes, Lucas."

A warmth I'd never known before spread through my chest and I smiled. "Yeah?"

"I'd love nothing more than to marry you."

I thought about teasing her and pretending that wasn't what I'd meant to ask, but instead I slid the plastic ring onto her finger. She surprised me by jumping into my arms and throwing her arms around my neck. I leaned down and pressed my lips to hers as I held her close and she sighed happily into my mouth.

"I love you, Lucas," she breathed between kisses.

"I love you too, Liv."

And I knew without a doubt that I would never stop loving this beautiful woman I was now lucky enough to call my own.

EPILOGUE

"She's beautiful," Mela murmured as she held my hand and admired the baby sleeping in my arms.

My baby. I was still getting used to that.

Shifting in the hospital bed to make as much room for Lucas and Luke as I could, I gazed warmly at Nate, Leah, Dylan, and Jason, who all crowded around us. Bouquets of flowers lined the windowsill of the hospital room with cards of congratulations covering my bedside table.

A bouquet from Derek and Emily, full of pink balloons with the words, "It's a girl!" floated in the corner. I looked at the people here to celebrate this new life with us and couldn't help but feel that they were my anchor in this world.

I thought of my adoptive parents, and a twinge of sadness passed over me. Things were still much too complicated for them to be there, but maybe someday we'd fix that.

Nate was joking around with Lucas, still squeezed in beside me on the bed with Luke on his lap, while Mela and Leah oohed and awed over our baby together. Luke gently touched the baby's head under Lucas's supervision, and he smiled as he said "baby" repeatedly. Jason squeezed my shoulder and whispered softly just loudly enough for me to hear, "You broke the cycle, baby girl. I'm so proud of you."

I squeezed his hand back, imagining a similar hospital room more than twenty years before with a very different outcome. My heart broke for the man before me, his brown eyes holding back tears. I thought of how he would have felt walking out of the hospital without me. It was unimaginable to consider leaving my daughter behind. I pulled her a little bit closer to me, as if someone was going to try to snatch her.

An overwhelming sense of love filled me for and from this motley crew made up of my chosen family, Lucas's family, and pieces from either side of my biological one. They were all here, and they were all mine.

LATER I WOKE up to Lucas still in bed beside me, humming a song I didn't recognize to our daughter, who slept in his arms. He kissed the side of my head, noticing that I'd woken up.

"What should we call her?" he asked.

I laughed at myself for still feeling like a schoolgirl around my husband. He gave me the beautiful crooked smile that seemed reserved just for me.

"Isabella?" I offered. I'd been thinking about it for months, though we'd decided not to name her until after we'd met her. "It means devoted to God," I added as an afterthought.

"It's perfect."

We'd planned for her and yet I still couldn't believe that she was here. Sunlight reflected off Lucas's wedding ring as he held our daughter tenderly and protectively in equal measure. This was *my* family.

Isabella stretched and her mouth moved as though she was nursing in her sleep, though she was in her dad's arms. I twirled one of her blond curls in my fingers, still marveling at the fact that she'd gotten all of Lucas's coloring yet looked exactly like me.

Tears pricked my eyes as I thought again of what my own birth must have been like. How devastated I would have been to give up Isabella.

Not this time. No, this baby was safe and sound with her own parents. She was not being thrust into the arms of a strange new mother she hadn't spent nine months sharing a body and nourishment and love with. She would go home with her flesh and blood, who loved her, and all would be right. Never would she have to wonder whether she fit in the world or where she belonged.

Lucas linked his fingers with mine, seeming to understand the range of emotions coursing through me without the need to speak. I rested my head on his strong shoulder with a happy sigh.

"You ready to go home, baby girl?" he whispered.

I wasn't sure if he was talking to her or to me, but it didn't much matter. We were both his, and we always would be.

WHAT'S NEXT?

WANT THE FIRST FEW CHAPTERS OF THE NEXT BOOK IN THE ADOPTED SERIES?

Sign up here to get sent the first few chapters in book 5 of the Adopted Series!

ACKNOWLEDGMENTS

Dear readers, thank you so much for being on this journey with me and enjoying my books. I really can't put into words how much it means to me when I hear from one of you telling me you loved what I wrote. You're the reason my author dreams are still alive so thank you from the bottom of my heart.

To my husband, Rob, thank you for inspiring me to write Lucas into existence. You truly are such a good man and I love you so much. To my editor, Cee, you are the best and I am so grateful for the way you push me to keep getting better with every book. Esther, thank you for designing my book covers. I adore them.

Once the Adopted Series is finished (if I ever stop writing it) I'll be moving over to write under my pen name - Jenn Wilkinson. So if you like my writing and want to keep reading my books then make sure you sign up for my mailing list at this QR code:

ABOUT THE AUTHOR

Meggan Larson is an award winning author, wife, mom, and adoptee. She currently lives in the Ottawa Valley in Canada with her husband and three children.

She lives her life around the concept of the starfish story, where a woman is tossing washed up starfish back into the ocean as they lay dying on the shore, and someone comes along and scoffs at her. He tells her she can't possibly make a difference because there are thousands and she'll never get to them all in time. She picks one up, tosses it back into the water, and says,

"It made a difference to that one."

Meggan wants to make a difference, even if it's just for one person.

Connect with her at hello@megganlarson.com

Jump on her mailing list for exclusive content, giveaways, and bonus chapters (fyi her pen name is Jenn Wilkinson):

ALSO BY MEGGAN LARSON

Adopted - Book #1 in the Adopted series

Fractured - Book #2 in the Adopted series

Reclaimed: Book #3 in the Adopted series

The Truth About Forgiveness (non fiction)

The Truth About Finding Joy in the Darkness (Anthology)

The Truth About Success (Anthology)

Being & Belonging (Anthology)

Starfish Stories, An Anthology Volume One

Excuse You? (A memoir)

Portraits (Anthology)

www.ingramcontent.com/pod-product-compliance
Lightning Source LLC
Chambersburg PA
CBHW020335310726
48979CB00015B/2373/J

* 9 7 8 1 9 9 0 4 1 9 6 4 5 *